Devoted

DELTA FAMILY ROMANCES #5

CAMI CHECKETTS

Birch River
PUBLISHING

Copyright

Free Book

Receive a free copy of *Seeking Mr. Debonair: The Jane Austen Pact* by clicking here and signing up for Cami's newsletter.

Chapter One

Esther Delta glanced over her shoulder but couldn't see the man who'd been shadowing her. She'd caught glimpses of him throughout the morning as she ran errands with her female cousins. He'd also been in a corner booth at La Hacienda where they'd eaten lunch. She was pretty certain it was Garret Thomson.

Garret was an attractive, seemingly innocent dentist she'd gone on a few dates with in Colorado Springs. He'd been a gentleman until the end of date number three, when he tried to check her teeth for cavities with his nasty tongue. Gross.

When Garret had called to ask her out again last week, she'd told him she wasn't interested in pursuing a relationship. He'd begged her to reconsider, certain they had a "once-in-a-lifetime connection," but Esther knew how to be firm and tell a man no. She'd helped raise five younger brothers and worked with a high percentage of men.

Her refusal of Garret was partially because of her duty to her family, partially because of the disgusting goodnight kiss, and mostly because she never went on more than three dates with any man. It was a policy she'd adopted during her sophomore year of college to keep her and any man she dated from a nightmarish experience. Avoiding love, commitments that were easily shattered, and months of debilitating emotional weakness was in everybody's best interest.

Garret had texted and called until she'd blocked his number. Then he'd resorted to leaving several notes on her car windshield, two bouquets of flowers on her porch step, and sending Crumbl cookies to her desk at work. She was grateful Papa had called and asked that she take a leave of absence from her job as an attorney for the Air Force to help her family protect the Delta secret. She was happy to do anything in her power to help her family, and a break from Colorado Springs and one persistent dentist was a great option right now.

Why would Garret appear in Summit Valley a day after she arrived in town and follow her around Main Street? It was concerning. Was he simply a man who couldn't take no for an answer? She'd dealt with more than a few of those. Or was he after the Delta family secret? With the stakes of protecting the secret escalating, the entire family was on high alert and everybody was suspect.

She caught his reflection as she glanced at the exterior window of the ice cream shop and shivered. He was across the street, studiously staring into Summit Valley's only clothing store. He boldly met her gaze in the window. His hazel eyes were far too ... calculating, making her think this wasn't a simple case of a man spurned by a woman he was interested in.

Unfortunately for Garret, Summit Valley was far too small to blend in and stalk somebody. Unfortunately for her, she had to figure out why he was following her without inadvertently giving away any information about the secret. How to draw him out?

Three men walked out of Blake's Grill, the hometown restaurant where Bailey, her cousin Colt's girlfriend and Shelly, her brother Thor's fiancée, were both waitresses. The men all wore khaki short-sleeved button-down shirts with Summit Valley Sheriff's Office logos, and black pants with guns in their side holsters. The man in the middle had a sheriff's badge on his shirt, filled out his uniform like a confident, tough sheriff should, and boasted the most handsome face Esther had ever seen.

Sheriff Reed Peterson. An ally and close friend of the Delta family. His deep-brown eyes focused in on her and the sidewalk swayed beneath her feet. Esther bit at her lip as her stomach did a flip-flop. Reed was a year younger than her, and she'd always thought he was incredibly good-looking and fun to tease with, but they'd never dated. Over the past ten years, he'd developed into an impressive, accomplished, tough, and tempting man. He'd asked her out multiple times, but she'd always had an excuse. She couldn't let herself say yes and fall in love only to lose him tragically. His career alone was a huge red flag. How appealing he was to her made him even more dangerous.

She was tempted to turn the other direction instead of giving in to the desire to scream yes if Reed asked her out today. She could share three incredible dates with the charming sheriff and then let him down kindly like she did all the others. The problem was, she didn't know if she'd be capable of walking away from Reed.

Would that be so bad? a rogue voice in her mind asked.

She didn't justify the question with a response. Quite often, it was better to ignore the opposing counsel's distracting questions.

The three men strode confidently in her direction. She knew Reed's deputies by name—Isaac Wells and Cameron Boyce. They'd both grown up in the valley, but Isaac was enough younger than her and Cameron enough older that she didn't know them well. She wanted to bask in Reed's gaze as he approached, an enticing smile tilting his lips, but she couldn't forget that Garret was lurking across the street.

Wait—Reed was exactly the man she needed right now.

In a very uncharacteristic move, Esther ran at the men, hoping none of them would pull their sidearms. She threw herself against Reed's chest and flung her arms around his neck.

His eyes widened, but luckily his arms automatically wrapped around her. It felt insanely good to be wrapped in the handsome sheriff's arms, but she couldn't let herself get distracted.

"Esther?" His voice was more questioning than romantic, but hopefully Garret couldn't hear him.

"Lover!" she all but screamed.

Reed's brow squiggled and shock registered in his features. She didn't dare look at his deputies to see how stunned they were.

She was making quite the scene, but she had to make this look real. If her ploy worked Garret would leave her alone or he'd reveal that he wasn't after her for romantic reasons and hopefully never attempt another dental exam.

Reed would understand. She'd explain … in a minute. Right now, she had to convince the jury beyond a shadow of a doubt that this was real.

She leaned in so close their breath intermingled. "Please play along," she whispered.

His gaze registered concern, but he nodded slightly.

That was all the permission she needed to press her lips to his.

Reed stiffened against her for half a beat and then caught up. No, he did much, much more than catch up. He surpassed her every expectation of what a kiss with him might be like. His mouth worked with hers in beautiful synchrony. She'd never felt lips like the good sheriff's before. They were soft and firm at the same time. They were warm and tingly. Like taking a warm bath infused with peppermint oil.

He pulled her in tighter, and their bodies molded as one. Reed took the kiss to dizzying heights. Esther forgot why she'd initiated the kiss, their surroundings, and any worries. All that mattered was Sheriff Reed Peterson. No man had ever kissed her like this. She'd never responded like this to any man's kiss. Not even with Roman. She and Reed could keep kissing until the sun set and she still might not be satiated.

A low whistle tried to penetrate their bubble of kissing ecstasy. A throat cleared. A loud laugh came from much too close.

Reed released her from the kiss but kept her in the circle of his arms. "You all right?" he murmured against her lips, his husky voice and warm breath making her want to kiss him all over again.

"I am now," she managed, blinking up at him.

He gave her an irresistible grin and her stomach flip-flopped again.

"Esther and the sheriff are *smoochin'*!" Bentley Jardine, a sweet man who was a little off, pressed his face in close to both of theirs and Esther realized where the loud laugh had come from.

"We sure are, Bentley," Reed said good-naturedly. "And it was incredible." He looked down at Esther and something vulnerable hid in the depths of his dark gaze. He wanted—no, needed—her to agree that it was incredible.

Esther wanted to shout to the world how incredible kissing Reed had been, but she was slowly coming back to reality. She hoped and prayed she hadn't made a huge mistake. That kiss had rocked her safe, organized world. She had plans, her destiny, and falling in love again was a question mark so far in the future she could barely see it. Maybe when she was sixty or seventy, she could match up with a distinguished widower like her Papa and help love his grandchildren. Right now, she couldn't afford the emotional havoc someone like Reed could make of her life.

Why had she chosen the sheriff to plant one on? It was dangerous to allow feelings that intense to overtake her. She could've grabbed Isaac or Cameron.

Except Cameron was married and Isaac was far too young for her.

Oh, boy. She shook her head to clear it and glanced over Reed's well-formed shoulder. Garret had slunk down the block and around the corner of the building, but he was openly glaring at Reed's back. Ice pricked at her neck. If Garret had a weapon, she had a feeling he'd be using it on the good sheriff.

"Esther and Reed up in a tree, k-i-s-s-i-n-g. First comes hugs, then comes kisses, then comes a baby in a baby ... thing," Bentley sang out happily as he ran off down the street.

Cameron and Isaac's gazes darted between Esther and their boss as if the two of them had jumped off the cliff of insanity together. Esther had to forget about that wowzer of a kiss and focus. She needed to get Reed alone so she could explain, and then beg him and his deputies to watch out for Garret. She'd share the information with her family as well. It was unnerving the way Garret seemed to know where she was at all times and the way he was currently leaning around the corner and glowering at Reed.

The only good news about this entire surreal interaction was it made her think Garret was just a jilted man, not a threat to her family's secret. A secret so important she'd sworn to protect it without even knowing what it was. Even if Garret appeared to simply be the ditched wannabe boyfriend, she wouldn't let down her guard. They'd research him and see exactly why he'd been following her.

"You're going to take me for ice cream?" she said loudly to Reed. "Thank you, sweetie pie. I'd *love* that." She lifted one hand off Reed's shoulder and waved to his deputies. "Bye, Isaac and Cameron. Thanks for sharing this handsome stud with me."

Reed studied her, trying to puzzle out what was going on. Esther was friendly and kind to everyone and she had a bad habit of using terms of endearment too freely, but she wasn't overly exuberant or loud, and she couldn't think when she'd ever used the word "stud."

"I'll catch you both later," Reed said to his deputies.

"All right, boss," Isaac said, grinning. "Have fun."

Esther smiled back at him, though her body was trembling. Whether from Garret stalking her or the adrenaline rush that kiss had produced and the after effects of coming back to planet earth, she couldn't be certain.

Reed kept one arm around her and directed her into the ice cream shop.

"Hi!" Taylee called from behind the counter. "What's going on with you two?" Her blue eyes lit up, thrilled to have a new piece of inside information to share with the town.

"Just one second, sweetie." Esther gave her a shaky smile, turned to Reed, and lowered her voice. "Can you text Cameron and Isaac to discreetly tail the tall blond man lurking behind the bike shop?"

To his credit, Reed didn't whip around and blow their cover. He pivoted with her, pulling her tightly against his firm chest and looking over her shoulder. "Blue shirt?"

"Yes."

"Got it." He turned her again so his back was to Garret. Esther wrapped her arms around his back and cuddled into him. Keeping up the act, or maybe that was just the excuse she was giving herself. Reed was the perfect build to wrap her arms around. He was thick and strong enough to make her feel safe and protected, but not so thick she couldn't comfortably hold on to him.

She also couldn't get her mind off that kiss. Maybe if Garret kept lurking, they could kiss again to provide overwhelming evidence. Her stomach filled with happy bubbles at that brilliant idea. As a lawyer, she was supposed to have infinite brilliant thoughts, but mostly she was a fabulous researcher and spent her days focused on compiling information for cases that rarely went to court. She hated going to court. Too many things were out of her control when a case went all the way to judge and jury. She'd called a judge "honey" on accident once. Luckily, the man had been her Papa's age and good-natured about it, but she'd been humiliated. She'd developed a reputation as the most thorough and competent researcher and usually other lawyers were more than happy to take on the court appearances.

Reed cradled her close with his left arm while discreetly pulling out his phone with his right and texting quickly. He pocketed his phone and bent down, softly brushing his lips across her cheek. "Is he stalking you?"

"Possibly. He might be after the secret." She looked over Reed's shoulder and shuddered. "He's gone now."

"It's all right. They'll find him. You just want him shadowed?"

"For now."

Taylee cleared her throat and moved impatiently behind them.

"Sorry, Taylee," Reed said. "One more minute." He looked down at Esther. "Name?"

"Garret Thomson."

"From?"

"Colorado Springs. He's a dentist. We went on a few dates."

His brow furrowed at that, but he pulled his phone out again. Still holding onto her with his left arm, he pressed a number. Esther didn't want him to let her go, but Taylee was probably already texting her friends, family, and her gossipy mother. Joleen would be composing a cute social media post complete with photos of both of them and set to romantic music: *The hot sheriff and the Delta daughter who we never thought would settle down to one man.* Everybody loved Joleen and Taylee. They were both dolls, but they couldn't keep a secret or juicy tidbit to themselves to save their lives.

Reed studied her while the call connected, his brown eyes full of questions. She loved the contrast his dark eyes and tanned skin made to his short sandy-blond hair and beard. His hair and beard both had highlights of red in them. Women would pay insane money for that hair color. She wanted to trail her fingers through his hair, then his beard, and then trace his lips with her fingers before she leaned in and kissed him again.

Oh my. She had to focus. She wasn't dating Reed and she most definitely was not allowing herself to kiss those intriguing lips of his again. She'd only kissed him to get Garret to leave her alone or to somehow discover that Garret couldn't care less about a relationship with her but had been using her, and trailing her, to get closer to the secret's location. Right now she'd bet on the former, but she couldn't be too cautious. There had been several deaths lately because of people coming after the secret and being willing to do anything to get it, including kidnapping, threatening, and hurting her beloved family members.

"Allie," Reed said to his office manager. "I need you to check into a Garret Thomson. Spelling?" he asked Esther.

"G-a-r-r-e-t T-h-o-m-s-o-n," she spelled out.

He nodded and repeated it, then continued, "He's a dentist from Colorado Springs." He paused. "Oh ... Cameron already called in a license plate number on him? Good. Clean record?" His lips pursed as if he wished it wasn't clean and he could arrest him on the spot. "Okay. Have them trail him, but no detention yet. Thanks." He hung up, pocketed his phone, and unfortunately released her.

She shivered.

"Cold?"

"I'm fine."

"Why don't we get some ice cream and you can explain?" Reed suggested.

The thought of ice cream made her stomach churn, but she forced a smile and turned to Taylee. "Hi, you darling girl. Sorry to keep you waiting."

"It's okay." Taylee grinned. "You look gorgeous, Esther."

Reed looked her over and nodded his agreement.

Esther's body warmed up. She knew many men were taken by her blondish-brown hair and bright blue eyes, and she received compliments often. It wasn't much of a concern to her ... until Reed looked at her like that.

"I didn't know you two were dating." Taylee licked her lips in anticipation as she leaned across the ice cream display case awaiting the spicy info. Taylee simply loved having secrets to share, and her mom exaggerated any information her daughter gleaned.

Reed grinned and took Esther's hand. He lifted their joined hands, brushed his lips across her knuckles, and made her quiver from head to toe. "It's pretty recent," he told Taylee. "We wanted to see how it went before word got out."

Esther clung to his hand. That was as good as telling Taylee to share it with the town. Her mistake of choosing to kiss Reed instead of someone else was getting out of hand quick. They weren't dating and though she would love to date Reed, she couldn't let herself. Esther had given her heart fully to a relationship only once. With a police officer to boot. She'd thrown herself headlong into love and thought Roman was her soulmate. She'd become obsessed with him and couldn't stand to be away from him. He'd tried to break up with her and told her she was "psychotic and scary." It had broken her heart. She'd called him repeatedly that night and when he didn't answer, she went to find him. She'd had no idea he was on duty and shadowing a drug deal. He'd tried to protect her and had gotten shot in the back. She'd been in shock and hadn't even been able to do basic first aid. He was gone before the ambulance arrived.

His partner had blamed her. His friends had blamed her. His family had blamed her. She'd blamed herself.

She was doing better now, ten years later. Her pastor had helped her find her Savior's forgiveness for the tragedy and helped her accept the fact that the drug dealer had killed Roman, not her.

After a year of counseling, her with-it and patient therapist helped her truly get it through her head that many factors had combined to make her issues explode. The combination of the breakup and Roman's tragic death. The pressures of college and wanting to get into law school. Hearing she was "perfect" from everybody in her life for years—parents, grandparents, teachers, coaches, etc. Even the responsibility she'd always piled on herself to help raise her five brothers up right, but she'd moved away from home and hadn't been able to help much, which had only caused her to worry more. Everything had piled up and become the perfect breeding ground for extreme OCD and panic.

She'd learned to manage her compulsion, break any habits that weren't positive or could hurt herself or others, and be on guard for signs she was falling back into that pit of rules and obsessions she couldn't break.

One of the good rules she'd stuck with was three dates or less before moving quickly on. In three dates, she could tell if there was any future potential. She hadn't found a man yet she was willing to risk more than three dates with. Mostly because she dated safe and boring men, like Garret.

She knew someday she'd have to trust a man with her heart again and trust herself not to smother him, push him away, or put him in danger, but it was like jumping into the lake in her family's valley in the spring and freezing instantly. She would avoid another relationship, and the pain that came from it all imploding, as long as she could.

Staring into Reed's eyes, she didn't know how she'd move on from him. As incredible as he was, if he was hurt because of her, or told her she was "psychotic and scary," she might need years of counseling to be whole again.

She tried to mentally slap herself. They weren't dating, for heaven's sake, and she was on top of her OCD. Had she just put him in danger by kissing him and using him to draw Garret out? No. Garret was the farthest thing from an armed drug dealer. The dentist wasn't dangerous or a threat to anyone, least of all a tough, experienced sheriff like Reed.

"Well," Taylee drawled out, "it looks like it's going pretty fabulous. If that kiss I saw out the windows was any indication."

Reed gave Taylee a conspiratorial smile. "Don't tell anyone, but Esther is more than fabulous."

Esther would've rolled her eyes, but she felt all lit up inside. Reed was just playing the part. Right? It certainly didn't feel like it. It felt like he was her boyfriend and would love, protect, and cherish her. If she could get more kisses like their first one, maybe she'd take the plunge into the icy waters of a relationship. Maybe with Reed it wouldn't be ice but fiery hot.

Fiery hot? The only thing that would get burned if she got too close to Reed was her, or worse, him. She had to remember this was all a made-up and momentary relationship. Esther was smart, analytical, and excelled at studying and dissecting the law. She wasn't the flighty girl who went crazy over the handsome sheriff and his hot kisses. She'd been the flighty, romantic but crazy girl once. It had resulted in an unnecessary and sad death and had devastated her. She couldn't go back there. Too much was at stake with the Delta secret and too many people needed her to play the level-headed lawyer she'd perfected for her to fall apart like she had at nineteen.

How could she convince her heart not to take a risk on this incredible man smiling tenderly at her? She had to stay strong. Somehow, she had to get her heart in line with her head. She'd put head over heart most of her adult life. She could do it again now.

Yet as Reed wrapped his arm around her waist and drew her close, she felt her heart give a shuddering beat and knew every part of her was in deep, deep trouble.

Chapter Two

Sheriff Reed Peterson slowly took bites of his butter pecan ice cream, not tasting it at all. What treat could compare to the taste of Esther Delta's luscious lips? His eyes dropped to her lips, but he lifted them to her blue eyes before she caught him ogling her mouth. Not that looking into those gorgeous blue eyes of hers was any hardship.

He had to make himself focus on some stalker idiot who was after her instead of dwelling on the hope that she'd given him the kiss to end all kisses because she was actually interested in him. He could *not* reveal his desire for Esther that was always simmering below the surface. He'd had a crush on her since he was fifteen and she was sixteen. Of course, as the younger guy smitten with the most beautiful girl in the state, he'd known he had no chance, but Esther had always been kind to him, and he used to think she flirted with him. Then he realized she called everybody pet names and was kind to a fault to every boy or girl in their high school.

As the years passed, she'd gone away to the Air Force Academy and became a lawyer and he'd graduated from Denver University with a degree in criminal justice. He'd dreamed of going on to law school but came home to help his mom raise his younger brothers after his dad passed from cancer. He'd worked his way into the sheriff's position, his brothers had both gone to college and were doing well, and his mom had remarried and was happy.

Any time he saw Esther over the years, they'd flirt and she'd call him sweetie a time or two. His heart would race and he'd pray she saw him as something more than the younger guy and a friend. He'd gotten brave as an adult and asked her out. Far too many times for his male pride to stay intact. She'd sweetly avoided or redirected or had some excuse not to go out with him, valid or not. It broke him every time, but sucker he was, he kept quietly trying. He had to try quietly because his mom and Esther's mom were close friends. If they caught wind of his longing, there'd be no stopping the manipulations.

He wasn't sure why Esther continually rejected him. He'd think there was something wrong with him, but women came on to him all the time, so he assumed he was attractive. He'd think Esther was dating someone else, but she was almost thirty and still single. So his hopes kept ramping up every time they interacted and he thought he saw a special light in her blue eyes.

And now this brilliant occurrence. She'd kissed him. Wow, had she kissed him. Reed had dated and kissed his share of girls and women, hoping to find someone to replace his craving for Esther, but no kiss had rocked him to the core like that one. Not that he was surprised. This was Esther. His dream woman. She was not only the most beautiful woman in existence with her golden hair, bright blue eyes, smooth skin, and full lips, but she was smart, fun to talk to, kind, and charitable.

They'd taken their ice cream out back on the patio and started eating the treat, making small talk about her family and his, until some teenagers cleared out and they had the walled-in outdoor space to themselves.

He leaned closer, wondering how to play this. He knew she'd

only kissed him to throw that guy for a loop, but he hoped she'd felt at least some of the connection, sparks, and warmth that he had. Could he convince her to pretend they were dating to get her stalker off her back? It would be a dream come true for him, but he had to be cautious so he wouldn't scare her away.

Was there any chance this stalker had something to do with the Delta secret like Esther had intoned? Papa Delta had given Reed scant details about a military secret hidden in the mountains above the valley the Delta family lived in. Reed would've liked more information, but Papa explained that even his children and grandchildren didn't know the secret. Reed was the only non-family member who had any details besides a couple military higher-ups and Thor and Colt's significant others. Reed thought that was probably from the necessity of him being the sheriff, but Papa trusted him and he appreciated it.

"What's going on?" he asked quietly. "Is this Garret joker stalking you personally, or do you think he's after the secret?"

She leaned in as well, and her soft lips brushed his jawline. Reed didn't know if that was on purpose or accident, but his body revved up all the same. "I don't know. I told him I wasn't interested in dating him over a week ago. He appeared in Summit Valley and has been shadowing me today while I went to a hair appointment, the bakery, the grocery store, and lunch with Maddie, Jessie, and Alivia at La Hacienda."

His stomach tightened. The idiot was probably after Esther and had no idea there even was a military secret. Not that Reed could blame the guy for pursuing her. How many times had Esther skirted a date request with some sweetly delivered excuse so she didn't outright offend Reed? Was Reed really any different from this guy? Not knowing how to take a no from the perfect Esther Delta? At least Reed didn't follow her around like a creep.

"So I pretended you were my boyfriend and kissed you to see

how he reacted. I was hoping I could draw him out and see if he's after the secret, but who knows?" She licked her chocolate ice cream cone absently, and Reed had to fight to not focus on her mouth again. "Sorry, I hope that wasn't a mistake ... the kiss." She swallowed and her cheeks turned a becoming pink.

A mistake? How could anything that felt that incredible be a mistake?

"What if he comes after you or hurts you?" she asked, genuine fear in her blue gaze.

Reed laughed in surprise at that. He didn't want to downplay her concern for him—he liked it—but she had to know how tough he was. He pushed away his melting cup of ice cream and took her left hand between both of his. Esther startled and glanced down at their hands then back up at him. "I'm not worried about a loser like that hurting me. I'd love to see him try."

Esther's generous mouth lifted in a beguiling smile, though her eyes still looked troubled. "The tough Sheriff Peterson fears no man?"

His only fear was that she wasn't interested in him. Which was probably true. She'd just admitted she only kissed him to see how Garret reacted. Well, dang. It stunk to hear his suspicions confirmed. He'd let himself hope she'd been scheming for a reason to kiss him for years. In his dream world, Esther had run to him today and taken advantage of the excuse to kiss him. Looked like that idea was a no, but he wouldn't let this opportunity pass him by.

"That's right." He gave her a cocky grin, still holding on to her hand. "I think your idea is brilliant. With Taylee watching us kiss and me admitting we're together, the word will spread quick." He could bless Taylee's wagging tongue for one of the first times since he'd been made sheriff. Her mom had unknowingly messed up a couple cases by spreading rumors. "We have to keep up the ploy of being boyfriend and girlfriend. Either Garret will take the hint and leave you alone, or he'll try a different tactic if he's after the secret. Working together, we can easily stop him."

Esther simply stared at him. Her blue eyes were wide and uncertain. "B-boyfriend and girlfriend?"

Reed couldn't hide his smile. She was disconcerted. Could she possibly like the idea? He hoped, given half a chance, he could show her how incredible they could be together. Yet if that kiss hadn't convinced her ... how could he up his game?

"And lots of kissing to make sure everyone knows we're together," he said in what he hoped was a charming voice.

Esther pulled in a quick breath. Her pulse raced in her neck and Reed wanted nothing more than to press his lips to that spot. Her pretty blue gaze blinked at him. Was she in shock or having a panic attack? He could easily lower her to the ground, get her legs above her heart, and then instead of helping her breathe into a paper bag, he could kiss her to calm her down. He smiled. Kissing her wouldn't calm him down at all.

Brown, creamy goo ran down her right hand. She startled and pulled her hand from his grasp, grabbing a napkin from the table to wipe off the ice cream and then standing and walking to the garbage and throwing the mess away. Reed picked up his half-eaten cup and walked over to the garbage as well. He dropped it in and turned to her. They were close. Close enough that her chest brushed against his. He was instantly filled with heat.

Looking down into her incredible blue eyes, he wanted to ask if she was okay with the boyfriend and girlfriend ploy, but he was afraid she'd say no or make up some excuse like when he asked her out. He had to stay alpha male slash in-charge sheriff and not give her an out or he'd probably miss out on any chance with her.

"Papa Delta said he set up a leave of absence for you so you could help patrol and protect the secret," he stated.

She nodded.

"Perfect. It will be easy for us to date, then. I'll pick you up at six. You had La Hacienda for lunch, so we'll plan on Sabores for dinner." She opened her mouth, looking like she might protest, so he kept going, "Let's dress up and play the part of a serious and smitten boyfriend and girlfriend." He could picture it now. Him in a suit. Her in a flirtatious dress. Him showing her exactly how smitten he was with her and not for any ploy. "We'll make sure Garret knows you're not available and see how he responds."

His phone buzzed, saving him from her saying no to them pretend-dating. He was on duty, so he needed to check this regardless. "Excuse me." He pulled it out. Cameron. He swiped it on, staying close to Esther. It was about Garret, so she could listen in. "Yes?"

"He turned off at the Juniper Trail camp loop, up Summit Canyon. We slowly followed until we saw his car parked. We stopped and hiked to look. He's got a tent and campsite set up. Looks like he's alone. Do you want us to stake him out and see what he does next?"

Interesting. Reed looked at Esther. "He's got a camp set up in Summit Canyon."

Esther shuddered, and he wrapped an arm around her. She blinked up at him in surprise, but it was what a boyfriend would do, so he went with it. He felt protection and desire well in him. This Garret would not scare his girl.

"Watch him unless something more pressing comes up. Thanks."

"Sure thing. Talk soon." Cameron hung up.

"I thought he'd go back to Colorado Springs. He should have work tomorrow. I can't remember if he takes Fridays off, but I know he's not the camping in a tent type. Maybe in a million-dollar RV." She worried her lip.

Reed pulled her closer. "I'll have Allie check into it. See if he's always closed on Friday or taking time off for some reason."

"Thanks. Sorry to get you so involved in this."

"I don't mind." Mind? Not at all. Esther was in his arms. He was in heaven.

She blinked up at him. Eyes that blue were impossible to resist. He started bending closer. Could he kiss her again? They were boyfriend and girlfriend, after all. Her words stopped him cold.

"It's disturbing that he won't take no for an answer," she started with. "I mean, none of them take it very well when I explain we won't be dating, but ..." Her voice trailed off, and she backed out of his embrace.

His heart was thumping heavily against his chest and her easing away made it ache. "*None* of them take it well?" he asked. "How many have you had to ditch?"

She met his gaze, and he knew she didn't have it in her to lie. "A lot," was all she admitted to.

Reed's gut clenched. Was his beautiful Esther just a heartbreaker? What made him think he was unique and could secure her heart where all others had failed?

She hugged herself and murmured, "I'd better go."

"I'll walk you to your car," he managed, strangely depressed. He felt like he was just one more in the string of men Esther had dated and discarded. It was even worse than that. She wasn't voluntarily dating him but had been roped into it by this Garret situation and by Reed pressing his advantage.

"Thanks."

They walked back through the ice cream shop, saying goodbye to Taylee who was still grinning at them, and along Main Street to where her Cherokee was parked. Esther turned and leaned against her car, blinking prettily up at him.

Reed had no choice but to press his palms against the sport utility on either side of her shoulders and lean in. His heart raced. He was going to kiss her again. He could claim it was for the fake boyfriend farce, but there was nothing fake about his feelings for Esther. She pressed her hands against the car as if to keep herself from touching him. He wasn't sure what that was about.

Anticipation to feel her sweet mouth meet his again filled him and he took it slow, holding eye contact as he dipped closer and closer. She closed her eyes, and he crossed the distance. Then she turned her head and his lips met her soft cheek.

Reed startled and pulled back. What was that all about? Why had she looked so incredibly willing, only to stymie him? Maybe she hadn't been willing. She hadn't wrapped her arms around him and tugged him close like she had earlier when Garret was watching.

Not looking at him, she ducked under his arms and tugged on the door handle. Reed straightened and caught the door, holding it open for her. She slid in.

"Thanks for ... helping me," she said softly.

"Of course." He forced a smile and pointed to the sheriff star. "It's in the job description."

Her lips turned down as if she didn't like that. He wanted to tell her all the deep feelings in his heart for her, but he had to insulate himself some way or she would crush him faster than an ant.

"I'll pick you up at six," he said. "You're at your parents' house?" Most of her family had beautiful houses up a picturesque valley ten minutes east of the main Summit Valley.

"At Thor's until the wedding. They're getting married in his backyard."

It was July twenty-eighth, and the wedding was August fourteenth. "Those two didn't waste any time being engaged," he said.

"They dated for years." She shrugged.

"Good point. If you know it's right, you should go for it." He stared at her beautiful face. He knew it was right. Them dating right now, getting engaged and married quicker than Thor and Shelly were planning. He knew she was right for him. Could he be right for her?

She only gave him a watery smile and tugged at the door. Reed had no choice but to murmur goodbye and shut it. He stepped back onto the curb as she pulled away. His heart gave a strange twist. That lady held his heart in her hands, and she had absolutely no idea how smitten he was. He was always decisive, tough, and in charge. He felt like a wimp around her, begging her to have mercy on his heart and return his deep longing for her.

His jaw tightened. Somehow, he'd have to show her how perfect they could be together. He'd been handed the opportunity. Now it was time to launch Esther Delta off her single pedestal and catch her in his arms.

Chapter Three

Esther's right hand shook as she applied the second coat of mascara and studied herself in the bathroom mirror. When she'd told Papa late this afternoon about the mess with Garret, the pretend boyfriend and girlfriend gig with Reed, and their date tonight, he'd smiled. That smile had worried her. He'd gotten serious and promised to check into Garret and any connections to Admiral Seamons, his close friend who might be leaking information about the secret or Commander Frederick, the militant leader who'd recently taken over Banida and was loudly proclaiming his rights to other European countries.

Stupidly enough, the United Nations was doing nothing to stop Frederick as Banida wasn't a member of the U.N. and Frederick had made lightly veiled threats about nuclear repercussions against any nation who tried to interfere within the country's sovereign borders, including attempts at humanitarian aid. Papa seemed almost certain Frederick would want the Delta secret and might be the one quietly sending people after it. She initially thought that was far-fetched, but yesterday they'd intercepted from the FBI a cryptic phone conversation between Nelson Palmer, the man who had sent his son after the secret and almost killed her brother Greer and his girlfriend Emery, and Frederick's chief of staff, a wealthy Englishman who'd defected to Frederick's side, General Carl Phillip.

Greer had killed Palmer to protect Emery, so they couldn't dredge out more info from him. The phone conversation hadn't given them anything, besides the fact there had been correspondence, which was worrisome enough.

She looked at herself in the mirror, decked out in the form-fitting teal-blue dress that Maddie had brought over to Thor's house half an hour ago. Her cousin had explained that Papa had said she had a very important date with their most trusted law enforcement officer. Maddie had winked and waited impatiently for details.

Esther had thanked her as she hadn't brought all of her clothes with her from her condo near the Air Force base in Colorado Springs, and she really appreciated the dress loan. She hadn't divulged any details, much to Maddie's obvious disappointment. She'd made the excuse that she needed to get ready. Esther was the queen of excuses; just ask any of the men she'd dated. She had no excuse to not date Reed now. The problem was, there were far too many reasons running through her head of why she wanted to date him. Seriously date him. That kiss had blown her away. Reed's solid goodness, ability to tease with her, impressive devotion to their valley and protecting people, and undeniable attractiveness only yanked her in tighter.

The doorbell rang, and she jumped. Esther wasn't the jumpy type. She had to calm down and be rational. She could fake rational. She'd trained herself well. Her work was always methodical and rational. Her schedule and even her exercise and eating plan were methodical and rational. Her ability to avoid seriously dating anyone was methodical and rational. Esther avoided extremes, obsessions, and excitement. People claimed she was the most even-keeled person they knew. That was a laugh, but she'd worked hard to break any silly rules in her head like every number had to be even whether the number of reps while lifting or the numbers on the treadmill when she finished a workout. She was impressive at faking sane and rational.

She could be methodical and rational with Reed. She said a prayer for help, slid into her silver high heels, and eased out into the hallway and down the stairs.

Reed and Thor's deep voices reverberated from the entryway. Reed stopped talking at the sound of her footsteps, turned, and stared at her. The look in his eyes made her warm all over. Thor glanced from his friend to Esther and chortled out a loud, obnoxious guffaw. Brothers anyway.

Esther loved her brothers. She was about as patient with them as any sister she knew, but five younger brothers could be a sore trial to any woman. Usually her brothers were ultra-protective of her and scowled at any man they saw her dating or even men who stared too long, but they all loved Reed like he was part of the family. Maybe Thor would approve of them dating.

But they weren't really dating. She had to keep reminding herself of that.

Esther couldn't even drum up the snippy words to tell Thor to stop laughing as she focused on Reed. His sandy-blond hair was styled away from his face, his deep-brown eyes were full of her, his handsome face drew her in, and he looked absolutely incredible in a dusky-blue suit, white shirt, and pale yellow tie. Was he seriously holding a bouquet of her favorite flowers and in her favorite colors? Sunflowers, daisies, lilacs, salvia, and gardenia in a gorgeous arrangement of yellow, purple, and white. She clung to the banister to make it down the last few steps without tripping on her suddenly unsteady legs.

"I thought this was a fake date situation," Thor said, his voice full of teasing.

"Sweet, honey, child," Esther warned in a low voice. "You back down or I'll tell Shelly about all the 'sturdy tricks' you and Aiden played on me as kids."

"Sheesh, sis." Thor whistled. "You may look like a gorgeous knockout, and you've got us all convinced you're a sweetheart through and through, but those nasty lawyer tendencies creep out sometimes."

Esther shot him "the look." It usually stopped her brothers in their tracks.

Thor only laughed harder and held up his hands. "I'm backing down." He grinned. "Love you, sis. You look absolutely beautiful."

"Hey," Reed cut in. "That's my line."

Esther went hot all over. Rational and methodical? She didn't want to be rational when Reed gave her that special look and made her feel incredible. She wanted to fling her arms around his neck and kiss him until Thor pulled them apart.

Thor chuckled and walked out of the entry toward his living area. He stopped and whirled, pointing a finger at Reed. "You know I love you like a brother, think you're a stud, and you can legally shoot or arrest me, but if you don't treat my sister like the angel she is, I'll kill you in your sleep."

Reed smiled while Esther blew out a breath at the threat. That was more reminiscent of one of the brothers she'd loved and tried to raise up right. Her mom and dad were great, but no parent could raise five rambunctious boys without a lot of help.

"Thanks for the warning," Reed said easily. His gaze traveled over her. "If I don't treat her like an angel, I'll leave the front door open tonight and a note for the FBI that my murder was well-deserved."

"Good man." Thor saluted Reed, made a heart shape with his hands for Esther, then strode to his living room, leaving them alone. Esther hadn't even asked where Shelly was. His fiancée usually worked until seven or was practicing for a rodeo. Guaranteed they'd be together as soon as they could be.

Reed focused in on Esther. "You are so beautiful," he said in a husky voice that made her feel like she had liquid fire racing through her veins.

Esther knew she was blushing. She wanted to tell him how handsome he was, but she had to somehow remind herself, and him, that this was all for show. "Thank you," she managed.

Reed extended the flowers. Esther inhaled the delicious scent of jasmine and whispered, "Oh, sweetie. How did you know?"

His smile made him even more irresistible. "Your mom sent me a text."

She rolled her eyes. Her mom. The entire family knew about the dating arrangement, but her mom had bypassed dropping hints and was shouting loudly that she prayed it wasn't fake. Not only were her mom and Reed's mom close friends, but everybody simply loved Reed. Not that Esther blamed them. There was a long list of things she loved about him. Not that she would share that list with anyone, especially Reed.

"Thank you again. I'll go ... put these in water." She turned and hurried out of the entryway and into the large gathering area. Thor was watching a lacrosse game. It wasn't their brother Chandler's team, the Boston Cannons playing, or she'd make him wait for her to watch.

He jumped up. "I can put those in water. Don't leave my buddy hanging."

Esther handed them over. "We're fake dating, bro. Fake. Please remember that." She was so good at fake; this would be a cinch.

If she didn't let herself look into Reed's beautiful brown eyes or kiss him again.

Thor lifted his eyebrows. "None of those longing looks seemed fake to me."

"I love you, my sweet baby boy."

Greer would've been quietly bugged by that. Aiden, Hudson, and Chandler would've loudly protested. Thor only smiled.

"But you need to stop teasing and meddling, or I'll kill *you* in your sleep."

He laughed. Loud. "Ah, sis. I know you were trained just as intensely as I was, but you're far too sweet to kill anybody in their sleep. Let alone your favorite brother." He winked cockily at her.

Esther knew he was right. She tried to think of a better threat. She'd already used the telling Shelly about "sturdy tricks" where her little brothers had done everything from putting salt in her hot cocoa to putting a snake in her bed. Maybe she should put a snake in his bed, return the favor. Except she loathed snakes and refused to touch them for any reason. Even to get back at Thor for a lifetime of teasing.

"And honestly, my beautiful sweetheart of a sister, Reed is the best of the best. Maybe you could take my advice for once, stop dating all those losers, and give my man a chance."

Esther blinked at him. "It's not real, Thor," she said softly.

"Then make it real." His blue eyes were full of deeper meaning.

Terror raced through her. She couldn't make it real. Her life had to be in control, and falling in love was completely out of control. Falling for an irresistible man like Reed would be worse than out of control. It could be life-ending. Some would claim she was being dramatic, and that wasn't her at all. But her one love had died because of her.

Reed laid out in a coffin. In his suit and pale yellow tie. Handsome and cold and gone.

Horror raced through her, and she blinked away that awful image.

"I'd better go," she said, needing to get away before she shared with Thor her fears and explained why she couldn't make it real, "not leave your buddy hanging."

Thor's smile drooped. "You're going to give him the three dates, then ditch him, aren't you?"

Esther's stomach churned. "How do you know about that?"

"I have eyes, sis, and we all worry about you." He gave her a significant glance and then the kick in the pants came out. "You can trust Reed. He would never treat you the way Roman did."

She backed away. None of her family had brought up Roman for a long, long time, and she preferred it that way. She thought they'd all forgotten about him. While they were dating, she'd made the mistake of bringing him to meet her family as she imagined they were destined for marriage. None of her brothers had liked him, throwing around names like "slick-tongued loser," "arrogant dud," and "pretty but pathetic." She'd been annoyed with her brothers not giving the love of her life a chance and thought they were simply being overprotective jerks. Roman hadn't been very patient with her or humble around her family, assuming because they lived in an out-of-the-way valley and a lot of them were cowboys that they were uneducated hicks. Roman had been a good person and a policeman dedicated to help others. She had loved him in her too-desperate, clinging way, and it was still ultimately her fault he'd been killed.

Only Papa and her parents knew how Roman's rejection and death had contributed to her depression and OCD and the horrific year she'd had recuperating from it.

She gave Thor a watery smile, turned, and clipped on her heels into the entryway. Reed stood waiting for her. She prayed he hadn't heard any of that. His gaze didn't look sympathetic or suspicious. That was good.

"Sabores?" she asked brightly.

He offered his arm. Esther hesitated before sliding her hand through. Warmth and sparks seemed to radiate from where his arm pressed against her side. Her hand and arm wrapped around his nicely formed bicep. Few men were built like Reed Peterson. It was a good thing, or she'd live in a constant state of heart arrhythmia. But maybe it had nothing to do with lovely honed muscles and everything to do with what was inside the man.

She swallowed hard and looked up at him. His deep-brown gaze was focused on her and a sudden rush of desire to never leave this spot was so strong she couldn't catch a full breath.

No, no, no. She broke away from staring at him and started toward the door. She was a strong, brave, independent woman, and she did not need a man. Any man. No matter how impressive he was. She had to keep her head on straight, get through the next few dates, figure out what Garret was all about, and then ditch Reed.

Reed held the front door for her and escorted her across the porch and down the stairs. He helped her into his truck as she wondered what kind of dim-witted woman could ditch a man like Reed. She'd always thought of herself as smart. Her teachers, her parents, other family members, church leaders, and work associates confirmed that. Right now, she didn't feel very smart. Her head was cloudy and full of only Reed.

The cab of the truck was charged with tension as they drove to Summit Valley and the restaurant. A good kind of tension. The kind that made her stomach dance and her fingers tingle. She clutched her fingers together to stop them from tingling and cast a sidelong glance at Reed. Was it just how good he looked that affected her so strongly? It couldn't be. She'd seen him in a suit. At church. Thankfully, she'd been able to control her thoughts at church. She wasn't doing so great with her thoughts tonight. She wanted to skip dinner and practice kissing him just in case Garret came around and they needed to look convincing.

Her face flushed. She and Reed would probably look convincing to anyone who saw them kissing.

"You all right?" he asked into the silence.

"Sure. You?"

He nodded. "Just ... nervous."

"You? Nervous?" She gave an unsteady laugh. "The tough sheriff never has any reason to be nervous."

He reached over and took her hand. A pleasant shiver traced through her. "No matter how tough I am, any man would be nervous taking the woman of his dreams to dinner."

Esther flushed with pleasure at his words, but then wariness crept in. Was he just being his charming self, or did he mean it? How could she keep her distance emotionally if he kept being so sweet and irresistible? What had she gotten herself into?

Before she could dredge up the strength to burst the beautiful bubble they seemed to be cocooned in, he pulled up to the restaurant. He squeezed her hand once and released it. "Please wait so I can get your door."

Esther smiled her agreement and watched as he strode around the front of the truck, looking tough, handsome, and ready to destroy every barrier she'd erected to protect her heart. She'd dated every type of man from courtly gentlemen to "enlightened" men who scoffed at chivalry. She preferred the gentlemen, as that was how her family had been raised.

Reed opened her door and smiled at her. She was in huge trouble. He easily helped her down from the truck and escorted her inside. The hostess was their friend Melene's youngest sister. Esther couldn't place her name and wished they wore name tags.

"Hi, Sheriff," the cute girl purred. All of Melene's sisters shared her exotic beauty with their full lips and smooth, dark skin.

"Abigail," Reed greeted kindly, but didn't encourage her. "Table for two, please."

"Of course. Right this way." She walked them to a corner table, handed them menus, then came back and filled their water glasses.

She gave Reed a flirtatious wink and as she turned away. Esther saw her mouth to one of the waitresses, "Smoking hot!"

Esther agreed but felt a little too protective, or maybe possessive, of her date. She focused on her menu instead of shooting sparks at the girl. Their waitress, Jenny, came and took their drink orders, then brought Esther a Diet Coke and Reed a raspberry lemonade. She took their food orders and their menus and then Esther had nothing to focus on but Reed's handsome face.

He gave her a gentle smile. "Have I told you how beautiful you are?"

Esther blushed and admitted, "Maybe once or twice."

"Do you think I could tell you again?" His deep-brown gaze was completely focused on her. A bulldozer could rip through the building and he wouldn't look away. Was there something else he should focus on other than her? There was. But she couldn't think of it …

Garret. Was he still lurking? He was the reason they were doing this fake relationship. Shouldn't Reed be on the lookout for him?

"Honey?" she murmured.

"Yes, love?"

Esther's body flushed. He could not be calling her love, no matter if it was for the fake dating ploy or not. Yet she'd just called him honey. She called everyone honey and sweetie; it had upset more than a few of the men she'd ditched when they assumed they were something special. Reed was something special, but not *her* someone special.

She could suddenly feel someone looking at her. "Shouldn't we be on the lookout for Garret?"

He nodded, still staring deeply at her. "Of course. Cameron and Isaac followed him from his campsite this afternoon. Garret is currently sitting in his car outside the restaurant. Pulled up right after us."

Esther shuddered and resisted the urge to look outside. *Keep it calm and under control.* So Garret hadn't given up and was following her. How had he known where they were going?

"We don't know how he found you here." His gaze slowly went over her. "You don't have your purse, phone, or anything on you he could've put a tracking device on?"

She shook her head. She hadn't brought anything with her, and the dress and shoes were Maddie's. "He's pretty good at keeping a bead on me." She thought about it. "He could've waited by our canyon and watched for me."

"True. We'll figure it out. Cameron is watching Garret from outside and Isaac is at the table at your ten o'clock to make sure you are safe."

Esther was impressed, and Cameron's position made sense as to why she'd felt somebody staring at her.

"And I"—Reed's voice lowered—"get the best job of all ... gazing into your beautiful blue eyes and holding your hand."

From any other man she'd dated, that line would sound cheesy. Reed was far too tough to ever be cheesy. From him, that line made her warm all over.

Was this all an act for Reed? Why wouldn't it be? He was acting the part as a friend and the sheriff. This was all on her. She'd grabbed him and kissed him today, then told him about Garret stalking her. She had to think analytically. Reed was saying all his sweet lines to play the part, but he was actually focused on his job and had his detectives backing him up because he was smart and covered his bases.

Of course he would act like the impressive law enforcement officer he was and make the fake dating scenario look real. It made sense, and it was in her best interest and the best interest of the Delta family secret. She should be very grateful to Reed for stepping up like this, and she was, but she was also humiliated that she'd let herself get emotionally invested so easily and quickly.

She'd allowed herself to get lost in his dark gaze and think all the touches, the compliments, and especially the kisses they'd exchanged meant something deeper to him. He was simply doing his job and being an incredible friend to her and her family, just as he'd always been. She was assigning deeper meanings to everything he did and said. While he so impressively appeared to be staring deeply into her eyes and complimenting her, he was actually doing his job and being hyperaware of everything. He knew exactly where his deputies and Garret were located. He was brainstorming how Garret could've possibly tracked her.

If he was head over heels for her, he wouldn't have been able to remember his last name.

She scoffed at her silly thoughts. She was thankful he was such a professional. That was what she needed right now. Not a boyfriend. She needed to be professional and in control like she usually was. She couldn't let herself get lost in him. It would be dangerous for the condition she had to manage at all times and even more dangerous for her heart.

The waitress brought the appetizer sampler and Esther graciously retrieved her hand so it would stop warmly pulsing in his grasp. She focused on the food and carrying on a conversation about how the legalizing of marijuana in their state had increased traffic deaths, violent crime, and underage usage. Esther did reluctantly admit that there was a state revenue benefit to the legalization and asked his thoughts about less police time and money wasted on marijuana-related arrests. Reed argued that it was a wash, as they had so many more hospitalizations and traffic issues related to marijuana use that it was hard to claim the legalization helped free up his deputies' time.

It was interesting and enlivening to debate with Reed, even about something serious. She'd eaten all of her yellow curry and shared a mango cheesecake with him before realizing the dinner date had gone exceptionally well. With the exception of sadly recognizing they weren't really on a date and the creep Garret was lurking somewhere outside.

"I interact with a lot of police and SF," Esther said. "You know the law much better than most."

"Thank you. I try."

"Did you ever consider law school?"

"It was my original plan." He drank some water and admitted, "But my mom and brothers needed me."

Esther gained even more respect and appreciation for him in that moment. He'd put his family before his own hopes and dreams. She'd taken the military route because she loved and respected the armed forces, because she wanted to increase the training Papa had instilled in her, and because she hadn't wanted a mountain of debt coming out of law school. She'd worked hard and everybody at home had supported her and cheered her on. She couldn't imagine being responsible for her mom and siblings as a college grad.

"And you can't beat being the hot sheriff." He winked at her.

"Ah," Esther gasped. "You've heard too many women say that, haven't you, honey?"

He shrugged, his brown eyes sparkling at her, but he admitted to nothing.

The waitress brought the bill and Reed smoothly put a credit card in and handed it back as Esther yanked her credit card out of her bra and tried to hand it over. Reed's eyes widened. He cleared his throat and said, "I thought you had nothing personal on you."

She held up the thin, plastic credit card, showing him both sides. "No way is this a tracking device."

Reed acknowledged that with a bob of his head.

"I wanted to pay," she said. "You're doing *me* a favor here."

Reed waved the waitress off with a smooth smile. He focused

back on Esther. "You're doing me the favor, going out on our first date."

Esther sucked in a breath. This was fake. It wasn't a date. But if it was ... Reed had no idea that his clock was ticking. Two more dates and she'd walk away. She'd fully enjoyed the conversation and being the woman the hot sheriff was gazing so deeply at and complimenting with his words and his gaze.

That was all. No deep commitments. That was Esther. That's how she stayed emotionally stable.

"Garret's driven away," Reed quietly informed her, breaking her from her thoughts. He must have an earpiece in and be the king of multi-tasking, as he hadn't slowed their conversation or broken concentration on her throughout the entire dinner.

She nodded, even as she deflated inside. She'd been completely invested in the interesting and stimulating conversation and she'd also let herself slip far too easily, assuming he was totally into her. He was only half there, focused on his job. She was both impressed and foolishly sad.

"Josh just came on duty and is following him."

"Sorry to add to your deputies' load."

"It's okay. The valley is pretty quiet, so they don't mind doing a little more than writing speeding tickets, dealing with stoned campers, and having to haul Clark Finland out of the Owl every few nights and throw him in a cell until he sobers up and stops hitting on the bartender or other women in the bar."

Esther shuddered. Clark Finland thought he was a womanizer and had said crude things to every woman Esther knew between the ages of fourteen and forty. She knew her brothers and cousin Colton had either thrashed him or threatened to thrash him on far too many occasions.

"Thank you for dinner," she said.

"My pleasure."

Reed was doing that entrancing thing with his eyes again, and she really needed some distance. Had his department paid for dinner and flowers or had he? What did it matter? He was on a job here, and he was impressively and smoothly executing it. She wouldn't be surprised if Papa Delta tried to pay for it all.

Her face burned, and she stowed her credit card back in her bra and stood quickly, shoving her chair back. Reed's face registered surprise, but he was out of his chair and escorting her to the truck without missing a beat. Abigail had to chase them out to the truck to get Reed to sign the receipt and give his credit card back.

The young hostess walked away and muttered far too loudly, "The sheriff smells and looks like hot man on a stick."

Reed was opening Esther's door as the girl said it. He arched an eyebrow at Esther, his gaze smoldering on her. Did he expect her to back up Abigail's words? She wasn't a flirtatious young girl. She was a successful lawyer, a captain in the Air Force JAG, and a Delta trained fighter. If Sheriff Reed Peterson wanted her to goo all over him like a teenage girl, he had another thing coming. She needed to act the part of fake dating like he was so exceptional at, but Garret had already driven off, so what did it matter?

She raised her own eyebrows at him, gave him what she hoped was a Maddie-level sassy look, and climbed into the truck. His hands around her waist easily lifted her in and made her wish she was still a teenager who could flirt and swoon over the hot sheriff.

They made it to Thor's house without her revealing how much she wished they could be dating for real and that she could break her three date rule for him. He helped her out and walked her up to the porch. He eased in far too close for her sense of comfort. Esther's back was against the wood and glass front door, and she had nowhere to go. Not that being pinned in by Reed was any hardship. He smelled delicious, like citrus and the ocean. Abigail was right. Hot man on a stick. Esther wanted to roll her eyes, but she was too caught up in this man.

He leaned closer and her breath lodged in her throat. He glanced through the glass sidelight and then let out a breath. "Oh, good. Your protective little brother isn't watching, so I can kiss you as long as I want."

He eased even closer as if to prove his words.

Esther could not catch a full breath. She put her hands on his chest to stop his progress, but that only made her more fully appreciate how well-defined his chest was. Her hand placement also made his breathing shorten just like hers.

"You said Garret had taken off," she reminded him. "You don't need to kiss me for our fake dating gig."

Reed studied her, and the entire world seemed to disappear. He leaned so close his warm breath brushed her lips. "What if I want to kiss you and it has nothing to do with anything fake?"

Esther blinked, but the vision of Reed's deep-brown gaze focused on her face and those words ringing through her head didn't disappear. He wanted to kiss her, and it wasn't fake? How would she keep her head around him if he kept talking like that, giving her significant looks, smelling and feeling so good, and being all-around irresistible? What was real right now and what was for his job and his protection of her and the secret?

Footsteps crunched toward them from the gravel road. Reed instinctively spun and stepped in front of her, drawing a small pistol from inside his suit coat. Esther reached for the door handle. She didn't have a weapon, but she could fight by his side. Yet it was always smarter to be in a defensive position. If it was Garret or someone else coming to hurt them, they'd be safer inside. Though she felt plenty safe with Reed's strong frame blocking her and knowing how well trained they both were.

"Reed." Her dad appeared around the line of trees.

Esther's neck heated up. Oh, great. Her dad was going to tease her about this one. She peered around Reed's shoulder. "Hi, Dad."

"Esther." His full grin appeared. "You look gorgeous, sweetheart."

She smiled and eased to Reed's side as he slid the gun out of sight. He glanced down at her as if he wanted to reach out to her, but he appeared to think better of it with her father walking toward them.

"Thank you, Dad," she said.

"How was the fake date?"

Reed looked quickly down at her, as if daring her to say it wasn't fake. What was he doing to her?

"Dinner was delicious," Esther said brightly. "And I determined that Reed could've smoked most of my class at law school. He's very smart."

"Well, we all know how smart and impressive our sheriff is." He reached them and shook Reed's hand, then kissed Esther's cheek. "Sorry I interrupted your moment." He winked and Esther gave him a threatening look. He laughed. "I'll leave you two alone. Let you get back to it."

Esther could not believe her father. He usually took overprotective to a level above her brothers but he, like everyone, loved Reed.

"Thor needed my help programming some automatic vacuum Shelly's rodeo friends sent as a wedding present."

Esther and Reed both nodded and eased away from the door. Her dad opened it and walked through, shutting it softly behind him. Esther grabbed the handle and pushed it down, opening it enough that Reed shouldn't try to kiss her again. Dang her self-control for being intact, but she had to rely on control or she'd get herself in a mess again. Especially if Reed was only playing a part like she feared.

"Thank you again for dinner and for helping me with the Garret situation," she said.

Reed nodded. "I've got some work in the morning, but I'll pick you up at noon for date number two. Wear casual clothes and shoes you can hike in."

Esther stared up at him. She knew she intimidated some men, even some of the tough Air Force officers and lawyers she knew well, but Reed wasn't intimidated by her. He was confident and comfortable in his own skin. She loved how decisive he was. Did he have any clue their time together was ticking away? Maybe he should stop reminding her what number of dates they were on. If he knew, maybe he'd say they were going on a casual hike that didn't count as a date. Did it matter to him, though? This wasn't real.

Yet he had claimed wanting to kiss her tonight had nothing to do with fake. He couldn't keep giving her lines like that. He was probably just another good-looking guy who always got a goodnight kiss after a nice dinner. She couldn't fall for him. She had to keep her heart safe somehow. Reed wasn't helping her in that regard.

As an independent woman, she should tell him he was too decisive and he needed to slow down. Yet instead of telling him he couldn't commandeer her time and her heart, she nodded and said, "Okay, sweetie. I'll see you tomorrow. We'll see if Garret follows us this time."

He didn't appear to like the reminder of Garret, but he didn't mention it. "Goodnight, beautiful Esther," he said softly.

Esther smiled, and she shouldn't have, but she said, "Goodnight, hot sheriff."

He grinned.

Esther slipped inside and shut the door. She slid to the side so she could watch him go through the sidelight. Unfortunately, he hadn't moved. He stared at her through the door, the heat in his gaze searing into her. Finally, he gave her an overconfident smirk, tilted up his chin to her, and then turned and strode away with a strut to his step that made her pulse race. She appreciated the view of him leaving far more than she should.

Mrs. Esther Delta-Peterson.

She let the name roll around in her mind as she stared at Reed. She liked the way her first name and both of their last names fit. She actually loved it. Was Reed only acting the part, or was he serious about her? She'd gotten lost in him far too many times tonight.

Horror instantly filled her as she realized what she'd done.

After every date with Roman, as she'd watched him walk away from her doorstep, she'd let herself think, *Mrs. Esther Delta-Lemmon*, and secretly planned their wedding. When she'd confided in Roman about the name in her head, he hadn't been happy about her hyphenating. He'd wanted her to commit to dropping the Delta.

It was all silly, but here she was doing it again.

In over ten years, she had never let herself do that again, not with any guy she'd dated. Honestly, she'd never been tempted.

How on earth had she let herself put her name together with Reed's? She was far too tempted by him, but that was no excuse. Was she spiraling? Was Reed too incredible for her to resist? She had to be stronger.

"What are you staring at, love?" her dad asked.

Esther whirled and blushed for probably the dozenth time tonight. She didn't blush. She was a successful, respected lawyer and military woman, for crying out loud.

"Nothing, Dad. Love you." She kissed his cheek and then rushed up the stairs. The putting her first name and his last name together had clinched it. She could not let herself for fall Reed, no matter how hot, smart, kind, and beguiling he was.

The depths to which she would plummet if things fell apart would leave her wounded and bleeding emotionally for years.

Chapter Four

Reed wasn't sure if the date with Esther had been incredible or a flop. For him it had felt incredible, but then she'd slid into Thor's house after her dad's interruption instead of kissing him. Had he scared her by telling her it wasn't fake for him? Possibly. Admitting the truth had seemed to fill those beautiful blue eyes of hers with concern. How could he show her how interested he was without scaring her away?

Thor had called him late last night to get an update on Garret. Reed told his friend the loser had sat outside the restaurant for a while, then grabbed a hamburger from the drive-in and gone back to his campsite. They didn't know how Garret had known what restaurant Esther was at unless he had been waiting and followed them. Besides that, the research on the guy was coming up blank. By all avenues, he appeared to be a successful, slightly nerdy dentist with a too-deep crush on the most beautiful girl in the world. Who could blame him for that? Reed could relate.

When Reed had said that last part to Thor, his friend had felt it was his job to warn him that Esther only went on three dates with each guy and then politely stopped the progression toward any kind of relationship. Of course sweet Esther would never hurt anyone, but it was disconcerting she didn't let a dating relationship progress past three dates. According to her brother, she hadn't for a lot of years. When he asked Thor if he could share with Reed why she had such a theory his friend had said he couldn't; that was Esther's to share.

Reed didn't have all the information, but she'd obviously been hurt by some idiotic guy in her past. He'd have to prove to her that he'd never hurt her and that he was worth taking a risk on. He'd knock her socks off with the three dates, and then he would soar past her three date rule and make certain she knew the deep bond they formed had nothing to do with that loser Garret or some fake relationship. He didn't think Garret was a threat, but he'd have his guys keep tabs on the man until he left Summit Valley.

He went into work early and dealt with everything he needed to by eleven-fifteen. Then he changed into a T-shirt, shorts, and hiking shoes in his office and rushed to the bakery to pick up the sandwiches, drinks, chips, and cookies Lori had made especially for him and Esther's date.

As he drove to Thor's house to pick up Esther, he checked in with his deputies on duty. Adam assured him Garret was still at his campsite, barely having rolled out of his tent. He promised to keep an eye on him. Carl was waiting at the trailhead to make certain it was clear for Reed and Esther's hike. He'd patrol the area for Garret or anyone else suspicious following them. Reed thought Garret was a joke and no threat, but with the Delta secret being what it was and not knowing Garret's intentions or how the guy had found Esther last night, he would keep her safe at all costs.

He parked in front of Thor's large two-story house and hurried to the door. Rapping his knuckles on it, he shifted his weight from foot to foot. He was nervous. Would Esther really only give him three dates? Who had damaged her and what had the deadbeat done? How could Reed get all notions of a fake relationship out of her head and make it real? More real than anything either of them had previously experienced. If only he could kiss her again. If that kiss yesterday had only been to distract Garret, he was in trouble. That kiss had distracted Reed from everything but Esther.

Esther swung the door wide, and he sucked in a breath. She'd been gorgeous in that strappy blue dress last night, and she was every bit as beautiful in a fitted gray T-shirt and black shorts with her hair up in a ponytail. Her blue eyes swept over him and at least she seemed impressed by his tough build.

"Hi, beautiful," he said softly.

"Hi, sweetie." She smiled, and he had to remind himself she called everyone sweetie.

"What's the plan for this big date, hot sheriff?"

He grinned and reached out a hand. "It's a surprise, but I think you'll like it."

She looked at his hand and hesitated. He held his position, praying she'd accept his offer. Tentatively, she placed her palm in his. Reed felt like he'd won a huge victory as he laced their fingers together. They stood there, just holding hands for a few beats, and he was ready to declare his devotion and his intentions. But she walked out of the house, shutting the door behind her. Reed snapped back to the present and escorted her to the truck, helping her inside. He loved the way her trim waist fit in his hands.

He rushed around to the driver's side, climbed in, buckled up, and pulled away.

"How do you know what I'll like?" she asked as they drove past her family's nice homes arrayed in the trees and around the lake.

Should he reveal his inside source? "I've got friends in high places," he admitted.

"My mom and your mom are far too good of friends," she said, folding her arms across her chest.

He made a show of buttoning his lips closed.

"Come on, what did she tell you?" Esther asked.

Reed chuckled and reached across the console for her hand. Again she hesitated before taking his hand. He didn't like the hesitation, but he liked the result. Her smaller hand clasped in his made him feel like he was on top of the world.

"First of all, I can't disclose the source of my intel."

Esther groaned and rolled her eyes.

"Second, maybe I was simply inspired and I know what you like just because I know and love you so well." His own eyes widened as that sentence spilled out. Had he really just said he loved her? At the beginning of date two? It was a rooky mistake even if the woman of his dreams didn't have some three-dates-and-done rule.

Esther stiffened beside him and pulled her hand away, clasping her hands together in her lap. Last night there had been a sweet tension in the truck as they drove to dinner. Right now, the tension was thick and uncomfortable. How could he backtrack? He couldn't scare her off and lose this opportunity.

"Any word on Garret?" she asked.

Reed wanted to somehow explain away his "love you so well" slip, but he had no clue how to do so without claiming he loved her as a friend or loved her as a sister and he wouldn't throw out either of those lies.

"He just woke up in his camp and Adam will keep an eye on him."

"Okay. Do you think he's a threat?"

"No." He really didn't. The only loose end in his mind was if the guy was somehow tracking Esther. "Do you?"

She shook her head. "He's a smart guy or he wouldn't have gotten through dental school, but he's acting pretty dumb right now."

Garret was smart. That made sense. He probably kept tabs on Esther and had catalogued little details in his head to help him.

They drove through Summit Valley and turned onto a dirt road that led to the trailhead on the northwest side of the valley, west of the ski resort.

"Have other men acted ... dumb when you ditched them?" Three dates. What was that about? The only good news about it was it had kept Esther single and given him this opportunity to grow close to her.

She shifted in her seat and looked out the window. "Some of them."

"What have you done to stay safe?" he asked quietly. He hated the thought of men stalking or bothering her. Since she'd lived in Colorado Springs for years, Reed couldn't blame himself for not watching over her. There was also the fact that they weren't a couple. Yet.

She laughed. "I thought you knew more about the Deltas than anybody unrelated to us."

He wished he could be related. "I only know what Papa shares with me. Not near enough."

"Well, I'll share something with you then."

He liked that.

"I'm a Delta trained fighter and the skills Papa and my dad and uncle taught me were honed by my military training. I could take down any man who bothers me ... including you."

They stopped at the parking lot of the High Creek Falls hike. He put the truck into park and turned to look at her. The confident smirk on her face was so appealing, but he didn't like the way she'd lumped him into the men who bothered her. "Really?" he asked.

"Really."

"No, I'm not doubting you could take me down." He would

actually like to see her do it. "You just lumped me in with the men who bother you?"

Her lips pursed, and all teasing disappeared. She looked him over and then said quietly, "You don't bother me. Not like ... that."

"Thank you." Their gazes held, and he was grateful that he didn't bother her like some stalker. "And I'd really like to have you take me down."

"Right here and now?"

His chest felt warm. "Sure."

She laughed and shook her head. "We'd better wait and use the wrestling mats at the gym. I wouldn't want to hurt you."

He laughed with her. "Good plan."

She looked out the window and said brightly, "You definitely had inside help on this one. I love this hike."

He jumped out and hurried around to get her door. Lifting her down, he said, "No inside help. I'm just that inspired."

"Oh, boy." She stared up at him, her pulse beating quickly in her smooth neck. "It's one thing being overconfident in your hotness, Sheriff Peterson, but lying about inspiration might get you a lightning bolt from heaven."

He grinned. "Good point. Your mom's my angelic informant."

"Thank you for admitting to it."

She eased around him and started toward the trailhead. Reed opened his rear door and grabbed the backpack with lunch and water bottles in it, strapping it on, locking his truck, and pocketing his keys. He lifted a hand to Carl in his Durango and got a salute in return.

Hurrying after Esther, he had to sustain a fast stride to keep up. He worked out every day, but she was in some kind of shape. He was out of breath from the quick pace and from the opportunity to be all alone with Esther Delta. Could he break through her barriers on date number two? He said a very sincere prayer for heavenly help from his dad to somehow win this woman's heart and a plea for forgiveness for being flippant about heavenly intel.

They strode up the trail, him trying to regulate his breathing so she wouldn't know how heavily he wanted to pant for air and her looking perfect and like some fitness model as she kept up the brutal pace.

After over an hour, she finally stopped and turned to him, flipping her long ponytail over her shoulder. "Is my pace okay?"

He choked on a laugh. "You're killing me, beautiful Esther."

She grinned at that. "Oh, good, honey. I didn't want to make it easy on you."

He eased in closer, and her eyes widened. "Nothing incredible ever comes from the easy path."

"Who said that?"

"My dad."

Her eyes grew sober. "I'm sorry you lost him."

"Me too."

They were quiet for a moment and then she asked, "Do you have any water in that backpack? I should've brought my own."

"Of course I have water. And this is my date; I'm supposed to take care of you. When you ask me out, I'll let you plan and provide everything." He winked at her.

Esther laughed. "I wouldn't hold your breath for that, sweetheart."

"Excuse me?" He pulled out two water bottles, handed her one, and took a long swallow of the other one. He hoped he didn't stink like sweat. It was a beautiful summer afternoon, but their valley never got too hot and with the shady trail it was probably only seventy-five.

She gave him a challenging look. "I've never asked a man on a date. What makes you think I'll ask you out?"

"Because I'm something special."

She lifted her eyebrows. "You're something, darling. That's for sure."

He loved her terms of endearment, even if she said them to everyone. He loved the challenging and appealing look in her bright blue eyes even more. Before he could pin her against the nearest tree, kiss her thoroughly, and prove they had something special between them, she gave him a sassy smile, turned, and strode off up the trail, still holding her water bottle.

Reed groaned, not so much because he knew he was in for another hour of trying to keep up on this incline but because of the interruption of what could be called flirtation. He hated that he knew she was a master at flirting. Could he be special for her?

He capped his water bottle, put it in a side pocket, zipped the backpack, and hurried after her. She didn't stop for any kind of break but plunged up the trail until the babbling creek became swollen and finally the waterfall appeared. It was beautiful, falling almost a hundred feet over mossy rocks. As a stupid teenager, he'd hiked up here and tried to scale the side of the falls to the top. He hadn't made it. Luckily, none of his friends had gotten hurt or made it either.

Esther glanced over at him with sparkling blue eyes. "Isn't it gorgeous?" she exclaimed, clapping her hands together.

She was gorgeous. Heart, body, face, and soul. He could only nod in agreement. She plopped down on the grassy side of the creek and hurriedly untied her shoes. Reed watched as she yanked off her shoes and socks and plunged her feet into the cold water. Leaning back on her palms, she closed her eyes and murmured, "Ah, this is heaven."

Reed's jaw went slack and his stomach pitched. He was going to ease down and kiss her full on the mouth. That would be heaven to him. Would she agree? Or was he just another in a long line of men smitten by the beauty, brains, and perfection that was Esther Delta?

He walked closer, slid off the backpack, and set it on the ground close to her. He sat close enough that their arms brushed. Her eyes popped open, and she held his gaze. Her blue eyes were full of him, and he thought sometime on this date he would get the chance to kiss her again. This kiss had nothing to do with Garret or any fake dating ploy, and he would make sure she knew that. After they kissed for a very long time.

"Get your shoes off," she said. "You've got to experience this."

Reed obeyed. He was always in charge and the leader, but not right now. He'd obey pretty much anything she said. Icy wetness enveloped his feet. It should've initially shocked him or felt too cold until his feet went numb, but his feet were tired and sweaty from the hike. It felt great.

"Heaven, right?" Esther asked, pushing her arm against his.

Reed looked her over and nodded. "Heaven."

She licked her lips. He needed to take things slow and be suave and charming, but his heart was racing out of control as she stared at him.

"Are you going to feed me or what?" she asked. "I'm starving."

Reed chuckled. "Of course."

"Sorry, that came out really demanding." She studied the waterfall and not him.

Was he throwing her off kilter? He was on shaky ground himself, so drawn to her he could hardly think straight. He didn't mind. If it was shaky ground next to Esther, he'd stand on it through an earthquake. "No worries. I don't want you hangry."

She smiled at him, and the earthquake settled. They'd been friends for a very long time and he liked and respected Esther. He needed to calm down and stop being a "simp" as his brothers would call it, angling for a kiss every other second.

He zipped open his backpack and pulled out a blanket first, spreading it out underneath them as she shifted to let him lay it out. He brought out the lunch from Lori's bakery and set it on the blanket as well.

"Thank you. This looks delicious." She inspected the sandwiches. "Please say the Italian on Lori's sourdough is for me."

He smiled and nodded.

"Yay for you prying information out of my mom. I was muttering about her being a traitor, but this is worth it. I haven't had Lori make my favorite sandwich in far too long. Thank you."

"You're welcome." He wanted everything to be perfect. Her favorite hike. Her favorite lunch. Would it make her fall for him, or was he just another sucker who got his three dates then was done? She was calling her mom a traitor for giving him info. That didn't bode well for his hopes.

"Would you pray for us?" he asked.

"Sure." She said a sweet prayer of gratitude and blessing on the food and both of their families.

They ate with the splashing of the waterfall as accompaniment. It was almost August, so the water had slowed down from the rushing torrent of spring or early summer, but there was still a decent flow. They were close enough that the mist felt almost as good as his feet in the cold water. His club sandwich tasted great too, but the best part of lunch was Esther. She was far too appealing and sweet, moaning over how good the sandwich was and then making a huge fuss about Lori's homemade Oreos. Her "favorite cookie." Reed thought he might get a hug for that one, but unfortunately she just thanked him profusely and slowly ate the cookie. He ate his oatmeal chocolate chip as he watched her enjoy the cookie.

As she looked to be done eating, she smiled at him. "Thank you, sweetie. Best lunch ever."

He pumped his eyebrows. It was so cute how she called everyone sweetie or honey, from a baby to an old, grumpy man, but he selfishly wanted to be her only sweetie. "Best second date ever?"

Her mouth turned down. Did she not like him reminding her it was their second date? Would she really turn him down gently after date number three? His gut tightened at the thought. He had to do everything in his power not to let that happen. But he wouldn't be a wimp and claim time spent alone with her wasn't a date.

He downed the last swallow of his juice, and he thought of an idea. "Have you ever gone under the waterfall?"

She tilted her head to look at him. "You can't go under the waterfall."

"Come on, I'll show you." He stood and offered her his hand.

She looked at his hand and then up at his face and paused. It seemed to be a major decision every time she held his hand. Thankfully, she put her hand in his and he pulled her to her feet. He almost tugged her in close right then and there, but he wasn't going to push his luck and get rejected. Timing, patience, charm, and execution were of utmost importance today.

With their shoes off, he stepped right into the creek and directed her up toward the waterfall. The rocks were smooth on the bottom but uneven, so they picked their way slowly.

The falls' volume and the splashing in their faces increased as they got close. Reed escorted her out of the river and along the bank to the far side of the falls. Closer to this side, a large boulder about thirty feet above them shot the water away from the wall. There was a flat stone to stand on, but you had to plunge through the side of the waterfall first. It would be cold, and the rocks were slippery and unpredictable.

"You okay getting wet?" Reed asked.

She gave a fake shiver and blew out her breath. "I don't know, honey. That water is freezing."

"Come on." He squeezed her hand. "My brave Delta fighter with elite military training who can kick her hot sheriff's butt isn't afraid of a little cold water."

Her mouth dropped slightly open. She might not have approved of his use of possessive pronouns. "You're baiting me," she finally said.

"You'll love this."

She hesitated a beat, then pushed through the water in front of him. "Cold!" she screamed as the falls drenched her hair and face.

Reed laughed and kept up, holding tight to her hand. She slipped a little on the rocks, but he steadied her and they kept going. Within seconds, they were through the sheet of water and standing in the protected spot. They were both soaked clear through. Water fell all around them, but here in this spot it didn't hit them.

Pushing the water out of his hair and off his face, Reed grinned at her. "What do you think?"

Esther blinked and wiped at the moisture on her face, staring around in awe. "How did I not know about this? It's magical."

Perfect. Magic was exactly what he needed. Inspiration and angels from above would be even better.

Please help me be the one for her, if it's right for her.

"It is," he agreed. He released her hand and slid his arm around her waist, pulling her in closer. She glanced sharply up at him. "I have to make sure you don't fall," he said as an excuse.

She rolled her eyes. "Delta trained fighter. My balance is unparalleled."

"Noted. Maybe you'll have to make sure I don't fall."

Water ran down her forehead from her wet hair. Reed reached up with his free hand and wiped it away.

Esther swallowed as their gazes met and held.

He leaned in closer. Heaven was so close he could almost taste it.

"Reed," she murmured, placing both her palms on his jaw line.

His stomach swirled. He loved her framing his face like that. "It's 'hot sheriff' to you," he said softly.

She smiled, and he kept easing closer.

"Esther." He stopped with his lips hovering over hers. This was their moment. He could feel it, but he had to make it her choice. No matter how in charge and strong he was in most areas of his life, Esther knowing how deeply he cared and that he was putty in her hands was important to him.

"I'm going to kiss you," he said huskily, "but I want to make sure you know there is nothing fake about this. I'm going to kiss you because I am crazy about you."

Esther's eyes widened but also filled with longing. He prayed she'd either cover the distance between them or tell him he could kiss her.

Instead, she did the exact opposite. She pulled back and released his face, shaking her head. Ah, no. His arm was still around her waist and the water hedged them in on each side, but suddenly their romantic spot was ... chilly.

"I can't," she said in such a low tone he hardly caught it over the rush of the water.

"Can't or won't?"

Frustration filled her blue eyes. "Can't. I can't kiss you, date you, be with you. I should've grabbed Cameron and kissed him yesterday."

His gut churned. "Cameron?" If Cameron or any man dared touch her, Reed would dismantle them.

"You're too much of a risk, Reed."

How was he a risk? He was about as solid and grounded as anyone he knew. He'd given up law school to help his mom raise his brothers. He was loyal to God, his family, his valley, and his country. He would never hurt her or betray her.

"I'm too damaged," she continued.

Damaged? She wasn't damaged. She was incredible and perfect to him, perfect for him. Something must've happened in her past. He wished she'd confide in him. He wanted to help her and protect her.

The water fell in uneven sheets around them as they stared at each other and Reed tried to think how to convince her that she was amazing, that he would be there for her no matter what damage she thought she had, and that they were meant to be together. There was no risk. He'd eliminate any risk. He'd do anything to be with her.

"I can't," she said again. "I can't risk going back to ..." She broke off and yanked away from him. She plunged straight through the waterfall, slipped, and fell to her knees in the creek.

Reed hurried after her, getting drenched and trying to reach for her. She dodged him and scrambled to her feet, across the rocks and back to where they'd left their stuff. Reed followed her. He felt helpless and out of place. What to say? Where to start? How to show her he would love and protect and cherish her if she'd just give him the chance?

She plopped down on the blanket and started tugging socks on her wet feet. It looked like a battle. Reed knelt next to her and put his hands over hers. She stilled, but as she glanced up at him, he could see the desperation in her gaze. What had happened to her to make her so afraid of falling in love?

He said a quick prayer and hoped he could reach her emotionally and not push her in the wrong direction. Tugging her sock back off, he took the blanket and rubbed her foot dry and then he slid the sock on.

She stared at him. Her gaze settled a bit, but she said nothing.

Reed dried her other foot and put her left sock on.

"Thank you," she murmured.

Reed nodded, still kneeling next to her. "Esther, can we talk about this?"

"No," she said, her voice cracking. "I can't go back there."

"Back where?"

Please let her open up.

She shook her head and looked away. Grabbing her shoe, she shoved it on. Reed recognized as soon as she had those shoes on she was going to run, and fast. He hurried to wipe his own feet with the blanket and tug his socks on, but her shoes were tied and she was on her feet before he got his second sock in place.

"Esther, wait," he begged. He couldn't think of the last time he'd begged anyone for anything. Besides begging heaven not to take his dad.

She shook her head. "You'll try to make me talk."

Reed gritted his teeth as he shoved his first shoe on. "I ... I won't."

"You promise?"

In his desperation to not have her run off down the trail, he agreed too quickly, "I promise."

Esther squatted down next to him and grabbed fistfuls of his wet T-shirt. Her blue eyes were as intense as he'd ever seen them. "You promise you won't pin me down and make me talk about my past and dredge up all the pain and try to work through it and all that garbage. You promise?" Her voice rose to a frenzied pitch and her eyes looked wild.

Reed's stomach was so unsettled he could hardly keep his lunch down. Had someone taken advantage of her? Why else would she be so intense and scared? He'd helped some victims after they were assaulted. It had been awful to see the pain in their eyes.

The only hope he had that she hadn't been taken advantage of was how well trained she was by Papa Delta and the military. Yet maybe that was why she'd gone into the military and taken her training to the next level.

"I won't make you talk about your past," he said softly, hating that he was promising this. He was an alpha male and a law enforcement officer. Those combinations made him a "fixer." He wanted to go in, solve the problem, and make everything right. His mom had called him out on it before. She'd told him sometimes a woman just needed a hug and someone to listen, not fix everything.

He had to be patient with Esther and not try to solve her problems for her.

"But if you ever want to share with me," he had to offer, "I'll be here to listen."

Esther studied him.

He held her gaze until her eyes calmed and her face relaxed.

She released his shirt, turned away from him, and started cleaning up the lunch and putting it back in his backpack. There was an uneasy truce in the air. Reed didn't know if she was going to ditch him or if him promising not to dredge up her past dating life and whatever awful thing had happened would give him more time to date her. If a miracle could happen, he would be the one to break through her walls, be the one to help her heal, and show her that he already loved her and would always be there for her.

Reed got his shoes tied, stood, shook out the blanket and shoved it in his backpack, then put the pack back on. His wet T-shirt against the pack was going to be annoying, but it was the least of his worries.

Esther gave him a forced smile and started back down the trail. Reed felt like the weight of the world was on his shoulders. He wanted to help her heal, but how could he do that if she wouldn't let him date her and he had no idea what she needed to heal from?

Why had he made that promise?

Chapter Five

Esther was an absolute mess inside as she speed-walked down the trail. Her clothes were damp and her shoes felt uncomfortable, but none of that mattered. If Reed hadn't warned her he was going to kiss her under that waterfall, she would've let him. He was such an honorable and good man, and she wished she wasn't such a mess. Reed had the power to take her under and make her fall in love like she'd never loved before. When he'd been so beautifully close and told her he was going to kiss her because he was crazy about her, her stomach had flip-flopped happily and she'd almost kissed him before reality had smacked her upside the head.

Instead of letting herself fall for him like any normal woman would, she'd completely flipped out. He probably thought she was nuts. She *was* nuts. She felt out of control, and she hated it. Would all her tendencies to hold on too tight and be needy come back simply from getting too close to love? She hadn't had a crazy, all-encompassing, trying-to-control someone episode like she had at nineteen ever again. She knew that was because she'd learned how to manage her emotions, but also because she stayed away from intense emotions like romantic love.

The terrifying thing was that part of her thought Reed would be worth letting herself lose control and fall in love. She shoved that away. It was too risky. The Delta Protection Detail needed her right now. Thankfully, Papa knew she would be a huge help to the protection, but he wouldn't make her Secret Keeper. At one point, he'd entertained the idea, and she'd begged him not to. It had to be someone who was healthy emotionally as well as smart and strong physically.

Most of her family and all her colleagues and friends thought she was steady and level-headed and reasonably not crazy. The joke was on her. Would Reed tell them the truth if he got past her barriers? Roman was the only one, besides her parents and Papa, that she'd ever let close enough to recognize how messed up she was. Then she'd clung to Roman like a monkey trying to make it work, calling and texting nonstop and trying too hard to be "perfect" so he'd never leave her. Of course he'd broken up with her and told her she was insane. What man wouldn't?

Reed wouldn't, a stupid voice in her head said.

Yeah, right. It wasn't fair to saddle an incredible man like Reed with issues like hers. Especially if she put him in danger like she had Roman. Reed's career alone should remind her to keep her distance.

She was fine. It was fine. Reed would just think she'd flipped out because he pushed too hard and she wasn't interested. She could convince him of that. It would stink to have to push him away, but look at how she was overanalyzing and stressing. She needed to heed the warning signs but it was hard with Reed being so tender and incredible. He'd said earlier that he "knew and loved her so well." Had he meant it? What did it matter if he did? She couldn't let him love her. It had been much easier when she could convince herself his interest was fake.

Falling in love and becoming a mess weren't on her agenda. Maybe someday, when she knew she was in complete control of her emotional and mental health. When the secret wasn't at risk.

She almost laughed at herself. Yeah, right. There would always be an excuse to keep from spiraling into addictive control. The secret would always be at risk, and though she knew she could stay on top of her OCD, she'd never be miraculously cured from it. It was part of her. She loved how her therapist explained that OCD didn't have to be a bad thing. Not only could every hard issue she worked through make her stronger, but OCD in particular made her driven, organized, and accomplished. Those were good things if not taken to excess. But as amazing as Reed was, she could see herself taking their relationship to an obsession far beyond what she'd done with Roman. Yet as she looked back and analyzed, sometimes she wondered if she'd trusted Roman. Sometimes her brothers' descriptors of him had fit.

She could trust Reed. He was solid, good, impressive, and loyal. If he said he was committed to her, he wouldn't run if she acted nuts. He'd try to help her through it.

Would trusting Reed make the difference?

As crazy as she'd just acted, grabbing his shirt and begging him to promise not to ask about her past, Reed would probably want to run the other direction rather than commit to her like she was already fantasizing about. He'd kindly get her home and then she'd only see him in passing.

Reed was a very kind person underneath that tough, hot sheriff persona. She could hardly believe how tenderly he'd wiped her feet clean and put her socks on. Her stomach did another flip flop remembering how sweet that had been from such a manly, confident man.

She smiled to herself despite her anguish. He was the "hot sheriff," and for a minute he'd wanted her. Not any longer. He was smart enough to know you couldn't fix crazy and he should stay at an emotionally safe distance.

They reached the clearing where his truck was parked far too quickly, and Carl popped out of his sport utility and approached them. "Good news," he said. "Garret Thomson packed up his camp and left a few hours ago. Josh called in a favor with a buddy in Colorado Springs and he confirmed that Mr. Thomson is home. Safe and sound." He smiled broadly at Esther. "Just like you're safe and sound, Miss Delta."

Esther gave him a watery smile. "Thank you, honey. That is great news."

It was. Fabulous news. No stalker. No guy after the secret. No need for her and Reed to pretend they were dating any longer. She risked a glance at him. He was staring intently at her.

"Bye. Thanks again." She waved to Carl and hurried for Reed's truck. He caught up to her, got her door, and helped her climb up. His hands on her waist made her long for more. She wanted him to keep touching her, keep flirting with her, keep wanting her.

Already, she was weak for him. Two dates with Reed were too much for her weak heart. He was too much. Too irresistible. Too hot. Too kind. Too smart. Too fun to be around and talk to. Too fun to kiss.

She put a hand unconsciously to her lips as he walked around, stowed his backpack in the backseat, and then climbed in the driver's seat. Heat flushed through her as she remembered their kiss yesterday. Their one and only kiss, and she had only initiated it to get a stalker off her back. She didn't regret it. At least she'd have the memory to cherish.

He looked at her fingers touching her lips. "You all right?"

She pulled her hand away and nodded. "Yes, great. Great news about Garret leaving. Perfect."

He studied her for long enough that it was uncomfortable. She forced a smile and said the first excuse she could think of. "Sorry, sweetie, but do you mind if we rush home? I've got to pee like a racehorse."

He let out half a laugh at that. "Like a racehorse?"

She blushed. "Sorry, a Maddie saying."

"Maddie's funny."

"She is." Esther adored Maddie. Everybody did. Esther often wondered what it would be like to be carefree, artistic, and adorable like Maddie. Esther had heard herself described as pragmatic, brilliant, and classy. She and her cousin were polar opposites. Esther was comfortable with those descriptors of herself and grateful most people didn't know how jumbled she felt inside.

Reed dropped the truck into gear and swung a circle around the parking lot. The silence was stilted between them. Finally, they pulled into her canyon and then into Thor's driveway. It was awkward to tell a handsome, irresistible man that you needed to pee, but it was the perfect excuse. She didn't wait for him to open her door, but jumped out and started for the front porch.

Reed hurried out and easily caught her. She all but ran for the front door, grabbing the handle and turning back to him. She found she couldn't hold eye contact. "Thanks for the fun date."

He nodded. "Could I take you out on Monday?"

She startled and couldn't resist staring at him. "You want to take me out again?"

He gave her a crooked smile that melted her heart. "Do I ever." He looked her over and then stepped in closer. He was so confident, so incredible. She had no clue how to resist him. "I want date number three, number four, number five ..." His voice lowered. "I want every date you'll give me, sweetheart."

Esther swallowed. Did he know? Someone had told him she only did three dates. Thor or her mom, probably. She knew they both loved her and wanted her to fall in love with someone amazing like Reed. Her parents never agreed with her when she tried to explain she wasn't just protecting herself but also the men who were interested in her when she limited their interactions to three dates.

She couldn't hold Reed's gaze. "You aren't obligated to date me any longer. The issue with Garret is resolved. I truly appreciate your help." Her voice was far too formal, but she needed distance.

Reed rested his hand on the door next to her head, and she couldn't resist getting lost in those deep-brown eyes of his. "Oh, Esther, I *need* to date you more than you'll ever know."

Her eyes widened and her stomach filled with warmth. He needed to date her. He seemed to be gone over her. Someday, could she honestly be Mrs. Esther Delta-Peterson? She loved the ring of that in her mind. *Mrs. Esther Delta-Peterson.* It was beautiful. She could imagine it on her email signature and her office door. She wanted to write it down.

Suddenly, her stomach pitched and chills pricked her arms. She was doing it again. Holy Hades! She could not be doing the stupid name thing with Reed. She'd cured herself of that after Roman.

"I need to ..." She pushed the door open and ducked under his arm. She had to escape, or she'd tell him he could have every date for the rest of her life. She'd tell him she wanted his last name hyphenated with hers. She'd kiss him and tell him about her issues and then ...

And then the smart, impressive Sheriff would withdraw. She'd start to freak out and call and text and hunt him down. It would be all over. She couldn't stand to think of the pity that would fill Reed's deep-brown eyes if he knew what was wrong with her and what she'd done to Roman. He'd stop claiming he needed to date her and seek a restraining order.

That would be much better than seeing him with blood blossoming on his chest from a bullet wound and her freezing and not saving him.

"Pee. I know." He smiled, so kind, so understanding, so dang appealing. "I'll pick you up Monday at five."

Esther should've stopped this. She needed to stop this. Instead, she let her scrambled brain rationalize. She gave other men three dates. Why not the man of her dreams? Had he really told her she was the woman of his dreams? Had he really said he was in love with her or was her frenzied mind hearing things that weren't there?

She had to get out of here or she'd push him back against the porch railing and kiss him. "Thanks again," she managed, hurrying into the house.

"I'll see you Monday," he said before the door shut.

Esther loved how strong he was. How he took charge. Many men were intimidated by her success, her brain, her looks, or her military training. Not Reed. He could stand by her side and be a man.

But he also wanted to fix whatever was hurting her. She'd seen that in his eyes when she'd grasped his shirt at the waterfall and demanded he not ask questions. He'd agreed because he was strong but also kind. He hadn't wanted to agree, and she never wanted him to know everything, to know what was wrong inside.

She took a deep breath and hurried up the stairs to the bathroom attached to her guest bedroom. Monday. She'd see him Monday. Their last date. She wondered what he'd plan. She could hardly wait. Would it be wrong to give him one more kiss? A kiss goodbye? Then she'd have to beg Papa for some kind of reassignment. She'd go to Chicago, shadow Admiral Seamons and anyone he associated with, and protect the secret that way. Heck, she'd go to Banida if her grandfather and parents would let her and go figure out a way to take down Commander Frederick. She smiled to herself, knowing her family would never let her near that level of danger.

She had to escape somewhere. She didn't know that she could

stay in Summit Valley and stay immune to the hot sheriff. Ah, Reed. For years, everything had been under control. Until he came along.

Esther Delta-Peterson. The words floated beautifully around in her mind.

She smacked her own forehead. What was she thinking?

Chapter Six

Reed about went insane the next day and a half. Simply adding up his credits and deficits, he was pretty certain Esther was not interested in him. He'd completely blown it by saying he knew and loved her on the drive up to the waterfall and then telling her he was going to kiss her and was crazy about her while they were under that waterfall. He was too transparent and too invested in her. He had no idea how to change. It was like he was finally getting his shot and he was blowing it. Should he have just claimed her lips and kissed her under the waterfall? He'd wanted to, and normally he didn't ask to kiss a woman because he could easily read they were into him, but this was Esther. If she'd been damaged by some idiot, he had to be gentle and move slowly with her.

He saw her at church on Sunday, but he'd only caught her staring at him twice before his phone buzzed and he had to go help with a mountain bike wreck up at the ski resort. Compound fracture of the tibia. It was ugly, and he was grateful for their competent paramedics.

Monday, he worked and tried to brainstorm what would be the

best date of Esther's life. Would she really ditch him after three dates? What was that all about? Her mom had confirmed with his mom that Thor was correct and that was the pattern she'd followed since her sophomore year of college.

He wanted to beg for answers, but he'd promised he wouldn't. How was he going to ever help her heal or discover what was going on when he'd promised not to ask? Dang it. Dealing with issues in his life, especially while on duty, was simple—fix the problem. If only relationships could be so straightforward. He'd try what his mom had tried to teach him, give Esther a hug and just listen, but she didn't even want him to know the issue. It was tough.

He had no idea what to do for this dream date. He should've taken the day off, flown her in a chartered jet to the beach, and spent all his hard-earned savings on the flight, a private beach, and a romantic dinner with an all-star chef.

His phone rang at lunchtime. His mom. She didn't even start with hello. "Okay, I've got the inside scoop on what might be Esther's dream date."

"You're an angel, Mama." He'd been praying for an answer and here it was.

"I know, love. You tell me that all the time."

He smiled. He adored his mom and brothers. He even liked his stepdad, though nobody would ever replace his real dad.

"She loves hydrotherapy."

"Hydrotherapy?" He had a vision of Esther in a swimsuit lying in a pool of water with a massage therapist rubbing her shoulders. Odd.

"On a trip to Cancun with the family a few years ago, the spa at their resort had an incredible hydrotherapy pool section and Esther went there every day, by herself if no one else wanted to go."

Okay. He couldn't fly her to Cancun tonight and his mom still hadn't explained what hydrotherapy was. He pushed out a breath.

"So how do I recreate hydrotherapy? Somehow I don't think the city pool or the Delta's ice-cold lake is going to cut it."

She laughed. "I'm all over it. So my favorite author of all time is Kari Strong, who is married to Gavin Strong who owns the ski resort and spa in Lone Peak Valley. Angel Falls Retreat."

Lone Peak was only an hour and a half away. "They have hydrotherapy?" he guessed. He could call the spa as soon as he hung up with his mom. Hopefully they'd have an opening tonight. He couldn't risk rescheduling the date and having Esther back out.

"Yes, sir. And the best part is I've emailed Kari many times over the years and she's such a sweetie. She always responds to my gushing emails praising her latest book. When Myrna told me about Esther loving hydrotherapy, I emailed Kari immediately and told her the entire story—"

"Mama," he interrupted. If Esther didn't want him knowing her past, she sure wouldn't want some stranger knowing he was in love with her and trying to break past the three date barrier.

"It's fine, love. She promised she wouldn't say anything to anyone, though she said she might use the story in a book."

Reed laughed at that. He could imagine a romance novelist riding a wave of creativity through life as she constantly drew on ideas and inspiration from everything she heard and saw.

"But because she's such a romantic, and because it's a Monday night and a little quieter at their resort ..." She paused. "Wait for it. She arranged dinner at their restaurant from six to seven, then booked out from seven to nine p.m. tonight for you and Esther to have a private, exclusive spa experience."

"That is perfect," he said.

"Yes, love, it is. It's also all paid for. You just bring some cash for tips."

"I can pay for my own dates," he protested. He wanted to pay and be the man and have Esther think he was the best man she knew.

"Of course you can, you prideful, awesome son of mine, but can you let me do something for you for a change?" Her voice filled with emotion. "All the times you were there for me and your brothers, with no one ever asking you to. You're the best. Let me do this."

Reed had tried to explain many times that he'd only changed his dreams and he loved being sheriff and being such a huge part of his community, but more importantly, he would never change the time with his mom and brothers and was only grateful he'd been able to help.

"Thanks, Mama," he croaked out. "I love you."

"I love you too. You know how incredible, handsome, smart, and wonderful you are."

Reed smiled. To his mom he was perfect. No way could he convince her otherwise.

"You woo that beautiful Esther tonight. I'll be praying for you both."

His throat got even thicker. "Thanks again."

"Mwah. Love you, handsome."

"Love you."

"Bye." She hung up.

Reed stared at the phone. His mom was the best. She'd been through a lot, and he knew she felt some guilt about him not becoming a lawyer, but that had been his choice and he wouldn't change it. He loved being sheriff, and family was more important than any career.

He was alone in his office with the door closed, so he dropped straight to his knees. He prayed in gratitude for his mom and for this chance to be with Esther. Then he begged both his fathers up in heaven to please, please help him win Esther's heart. He forced himself to add, if it was best for her and in Heavenly Father's plans for both of them, but then he was back to begging, *Please, please let Esther falling in love with me be thy will.*

He would've smiled at his begging to bend heaven's will to his, if he wasn't so desperate to have the dream of him and Esther come true.

Chapter Seven

Reed had texted asking if four-thirty was all right to pick her up. Esther was tempted to tell him she couldn't go tonight, but she wanted this last date with him far too much. She responded she'd be ready and asked what to wear. He said whatever she wanted to wear for a nice dinner and to please pack a swimsuit and any girl stuff she needed for after they swam.

She smiled. Girl stuff. He was cute. No, Reed was far beyond cute.

At four-twenty-six, she had a small bag packed, was wearing a sleeveless white summer dress, and was bouncing from heel to toe in Thor's entryway, peering out the sidelight and listening for a certain sheriff's truck. She hoped to get out of the house before Thor came inside. He worked with his broncs most days, training them to throw cowboys off their backs in rodeos.

The back door opened, and she stiffened. She loved Thor, but she didn't want any brotherly interruptions or teasing before her date or, even worse, him teasing her and Reed once he came for her.

"Sis?" Thor called.

"In here," she said in a resigned tone.

He hurried through his house and into the entryway. He was dusty in a T-shirt, jeans, and boots, and his matted down hair showed he'd just removed his hat. He usually took off his boots when he came inside, but he was obviously in a hurry.

"Oh, good. I was afraid I'd miss you when I heard you were going at four-thirty instead of five."

Esther shook her head. Might as well just post the details of their date on the Summit Valley Facebook page. Maybe Taylee or her mom already had. "Reed or Mom?"

"Mom." He smiled. "Now, I know you don't want advice from your little brother."

She nodded. "Definitely not."

"But I'm going to give it to you."

"Does Shelly ever tell you that you're pigheaded and too determined?"

"All the time." He barely paused for a breath. "A couple months ago, Shelly got it all mixed up in her head that she wasn't worthy of me and tried to push me away."

Esther startled. She'd watched her brother and Shelly's relationship over the years. Shelly always had a smile on her face, and she also had a lot of pride. She didn't know Shelly hadn't thought of herself as worthy of Thor, but she knew they'd had a rocky patch before they got engaged.

"She gave me permission to tell you that," he said quickly. "And I'm not saying that's how you feel, but I worry. All this three-dates-and-the-dude-is-done deal and never dating the caliber of men worthy of *you*, until Reed."

Esther wished Thor didn't know so much and observe so well. He wasn't observant enough to know about her emotional issues, but she hid them very well.

"I'm thinking it stems back to that idiot Roman dumping you

71

and then getting shot. I'm not trying to speak ill of the dead, but Roman was too slick and not committed enough to you and the fact is it was a drug dealer's fault Roman died, not yours."

Thor was always direct, but he wasn't pulling punches tonight.

Thor looked into her eyes. "You're enough, sis. You're more than enough. Any man would be honored and blessed to have you love him."

Esther swallowed. His words meant a lot, but he had no clue about her OCD and how crazy she became with Roman. His death was on her head, and she'd watched him die. She knew her parents and Papa wouldn't betray that confidence.

"I don't know what issues you have or think you have," he said. "But honestly, Esther, we all have some kind of issue."

Esther rocked back on her heels. Maybe he did see what she thought she hid. She thought about his statement. She supposed it could be true. Everybody had some kind of demon they fought or facet about themselves emotionally, physically, or spiritually that they wanted to change. But did Thor or Shelly have huge issues like she did? She doubted it.

"All I'm saying is, please give Reed a chance. He's the best of the best." He waited as if she'd agree.

A truck motor sounded in the drive.

"Reed," she said, putting a hand to her stomach, suddenly breathless.

Thor's face broke into a huge grin. Her brother was so cute. "You love him. I can see it in your face."

"I don't love him," she protested fiercely.

Thor reached for her, but then stopped. "Sorry, I want to hug you, but I'll dirty up your pretty dress. You're amazing, sis. Go tonight and just have fun. Enjoy Reed, enjoy the experience, don't think about the future, just see how it goes and how you feel."

Footsteps and then a rap at the door.

Esther eased close to Thor and cautiously kissed his cheek. "Love you," she said, not admitting to or agreeing with anything but really appreciating his intervention attempt. If only her issues weren't so huge and could be resolved by some kind words from a well-meaning brother. Then again, if it was that simple, her issues wouldn't have necessitated so much caution and personal control for the last decade.

"Love you." He lifted a hand, turned, and strode away, giving her privacy to greet Reed. If only she could take advantage of that privacy and kiss Reed hello.

Her cheeks were flushed as she turned and swung the door wide. Reed stood there, looking incredible in a pale blue Henley shirt and dark wash jeans. His deep brown eyes swept over her and he said huskily, "Hey, beautiful."

She smiled and tucked her hair behind her ear. "Hi, hot sheriff."

He grinned and extended his hand. Esther hesitated. She wished she hadn't as his eyes reflected the sting of her not being able to just place her hand in his, to not just instinctively trust him with her hand, but it was deeper than that for her. Placing her hand in his so unconsciously was like trusting him with her heart. She wasn't ready to make that leap and didn't know if she'd ever be.

Tentatively, she placed her palm against his. Warm tingles slid along her hand as their palms aligned. She thought he'd clasp her hand tight, but he waited. Reed had offered his hand, and it was symbolic as if he were offering her his heart. Her own heart raced, not sure if she should make the next move.

Reed was patient and confident enough to not push her. Like him asking if he could kiss her behind the waterfall instead of just going for it. She loved that about him.

He gave her a gentle smile, and she thought of Thor's words. Not all the stuff about Shelly struggling to think she was worthy of Thor, or Thor claiming Esther was more than enough and any man would be blessed to have her love him—that would take a little more time and thought. She focused on his advice to enjoy tonight and not think too much about the future. It was a hard ask for someone who never let herself turn off that worry.

She laced their fingers together, and Reed gave her a smile that said she'd made him very happy. How could she possibly resist the hot sheriff? Especially because Reed was so much more to her than his beautiful exterior.

She pushed the worries away and focused on enjoying the moment. One struggle with her disorder was trying to live in the moment and not always plotting, planning, controlling, and being prepared for whatever was coming next. Reed deserved so much from her that she couldn't give, but she could give him her focus and her attention on this one date.

He reached out his other hand, and she didn't know if he wanted to hold both of her hands, but then he reached up and slid her bag off her shoulder. She smiled her thanks. He walked her to his truck, the silence between them comfortable yet sparkling with possibility. He helped her in, put her bag in the back, and then hurried around to the driver's seat.

She turned to him and felt like a little kid as she asked excitedly, "Where are we going?"

"It's a surprise."

"Hmm. Can I guess?"

"You can try."

Esther didn't get many surprises in her busy life. She generally didn't love the unknown because she couldn't control it. But instinctively, she trusted Reed to plan something she would love. Maybe she already trusted him more than she realized.

They drove out of Thor's driveway, and she started guessing. "Kayaking or paddle boarding on the lake?"

"No, ma'am."

"Hmm. We're going to find another waterfall?" Her cheeks burned as she thought of their last waterfall experience. It had been incredible, but she'd almost messed it up by getting so intense and grabbing his shirt and demanding he not ask questions like she had. Thankfully, Reed didn't seem upset by any of it. He'd seemed bothered she wouldn't let him help her, but he hadn't pushed.

She held up one of her sandaled feet. "I might not be very good at hiking in these things."

He chuckled and extended his hand across the console. Esther wrapped her hand around it without thinking, making him grin as if he'd won the lottery. She smiled back. Listening to Thor and simply enjoying this date was going well.

"No hiking or freezing waterfalls."

"But you had me bring the swimsuit. And wear a dress for dinner. Hmm."

They drove through Summit Valley and toward the southern canyon that led out of the valley, and she started guessing anything she could think of in Denver that had to do with water, including her performing with the professional divers at Casa Bonita. He'd laugh, tease, or squeeze her hand every time. When she guessed tubing the river in Golden, a town west of Denver, he said they'd do that one soon.

That led to her telling him about some Air Force cadets who'd kayaked that river when it was full of spring runoff and gotten badly injured. They'd had a couple seventeen-year-old girls with them and one of the girls' parents had sued the Air Force. They talked about the case and all the research she'd done for it as they drove the highway and then entered a gorgeous valley over an hour north of theirs. Esther loved talking law with Reed. He was more insightful and knowledgeable than a lot of the lawyers she knew.

The valley they drove into stole their attention. It was almost as beautiful as Summit Valley, green and lush with an adorable downtown and a blue ribbon of river snaking around the green valley floor. They drove to the far north end toward the ski resort. "Angel Falls Retreat," she read the sign. "You *are* taking me to a waterfall."

He parked next to the huge, gorgeous lodge and lifted their clasped hands to his lips, brushing his mouth over her knuckles. She instantly heated up. "Nope. I'm going to feed you before you put your swimsuit on, but you can keep guessing."

The lodge was even prettier on the inside, with two story-windows and views of the valley below. The restaurant was on the back side and had views of the green mountain and ski resort. There were a few mountain bikers riding down the trails and a family and another couple in the restaurant, but it was pretty quiet.

A hostess greeted them and when she heard Reed's name on the reservation, her smile grew. "It's a pleasure to have you here," she said to both of them. She led them to a quiet table next to a large window and sat them down, bringing them waters and menus.

Their waitress hustled over quickly and introduced herself as Mary. She got their drink orders and made recommendations. As she rushed away to get their drinks, she almost ran into a tall, beautiful blonde lady. They exchanged greetings and a quick hug.

The blonde walked to their table, beamed at them, and clasped her hands together, bouncing on her heels. "I'm Kari Strong. It's wonderful to meet you, Reed and Esther."

Reed quickly stood and extended his hand. "Nice to meet you, Kari. Thank you so much for setting all of this up."

"Oh, it's my pleasure, believe me." She winked at Esther. "I just had to meet you both; get some inspiration, you see."

Esther wasn't sure what that meant. Inspiration for what?

Kari leaned in. "I'm a romance novelist," she said conspiratorially.

Esther smiled, still at a loss. Did that mean she was going to write about them? What did she think she knew about them?

Kari turned back to Reed. "Everything is ready for you. Enjoy your dinner, then I'll meet you at the spa and show you around."

Esther grinned. A spa. Cool.

"Thank you." Reed waved.

Kari waved both hands happily and then turned and walked away.

Reed sat back down.

"A spa?" Esther asked.

He smiled. "The opportunity to cross examine the witness has passed. Sorry."

She laughed.

They ordered and chatted easily throughout dinner. As they finished, he left a tip, but they never brought a bill. He escorted her back outside and got their bags out of the truck. They walked a short distance to a building labeled "The Spa."

Reed held the door for her, and they walked in. Kari sat at a desk, tapping away on a laptop. She glanced up, removed her glasses, and jumped to her feet. "Yay, you're here! I'm so excited about this. Can I just ask one favor?"

"Sure." Reed nodded.

"If you get married, can I come to the wedding to complete the story arc?"

Esther froze and wondered if this beautiful lady was a bit on the crazy side. But who was she to judge? Esther personally chose to hide her crazy. This lady was clearly more in touch with her crazy—she owned it.

Reed held up a hand. "Slow down a bit so we don't scare her away." His voice was good-natured, but also tight. He was legitimately worried about scaring Esther away. She'd been relaxed and enjoyed the evening so far. *Stay in the moment and don't stress*, she begged herself. Inside, she was stressing triple time and she also could see in a beautiful script: *Esther Delta-Peterson*. Ah, no. Push it away.

"Oh, gotcha. Sorry." Kari looked them over. "But I do have to say you two are both gorgeous and I can see a lot of depth and character as well. Great light in each of your eyes." She nodded, her own blue eyes glinting mischievously. "You're a fabulous match, for sure. You both understand it's not about finding the perfect person. It's about finding the *right* person that you can love, grow, and sacrifice with and for." She smiled as if she'd just given them the Holy Grail.

They both shifted uneasily. Esther liked what she'd said. Nobody was perfect, but each person could find the right fit for them and grow together with their partner. Interesting.

"I'd better stop. Let me show you the facility, then I'll lock the front doors and you can stay as long as you want. You'll have the facility all to yourselves. Just make sure the door shuts behind you when you leave. Liability and all that." She waved a hand as if liability was the furthest thing from her mind. She and Esther definitely lived in different worlds. "Oh, and if you remember, shut the lights off." She shrugged. "My husband worries about stuff like that."

Esther wondered if this beautiful blonde had any worries. How would that be to let your husband take the worries for you? She snuck a glance at Reed as Kari walked away from them. He was straight, strong, true, and loyal. He'd be an incredible husband for some lucky girl and try to ease or take away any worries he could, shoulder the burdens of life together. He glanced at her and smiled softly, his dark eyes lit up. Esther was entranced by his dark gaze and let herself fantasize for just a moment that she was the woman Reed would love, cherish, and bear the burdens of life with. Getting lost in that fantasy almost felt like therapy, and for a brief second that stretched and stretched, she wondered if it could actually work. *Esther Delta-Peterson*. It wasn't scary, but beautiful.

A door banged open.

"This is the women's entrance ... Oh!"

Esther forced herself to look at Kari standing by the woman's locker room instead of Reed. The woman's blue eyes were sparkling. "You two are so textbook." Kari let the door go and clapped her hands together. "Ah, the beautiful tension lighting up the air between you. The way you're staring at each other as if there isn't another person in this world. Yay! I'm so in love with you both and your story."

Esther had no clue what to say to that. Reed put his hand on her lower back and escorted her to the women's entrance. "I'll go through the men's and meet you?" he said to Kari.

"Yes, sir." The woman smiled hugely. "Actually, change into your suit and I can get you started on the therapies and then show you the stuff you can do on your own. Usually we'd have an attendant with you at all times..." She lowered her voice. "My husband would actually prefer that, more of the liability nonsense, but Heather and I felt alone time was more important." She winked, swung the door wide, and waited for Esther to walk through.

She walked Esther through the beautiful locker room, showing her the showers and the complimentary skin and hair products and the private hot tubs for those who preferred that. Once Esther had changed into her suit, Kari gave her a plush robe and slippers from a locker.

They walked toward another exit and Esther thought she might escape a private interrogation by this very open and friendly author, but Kari stopped and turned to her. "So if you don't mind me asking —for research, you see—how did you know Reed was the love of your life?"

Esther's eyes widened. She clutched the robe straps and shook her head. "Kari. This is only our third date." *And last,* but she left that part out. "Who told you he was the love of my life?"

"Oh." Kari's eyes registered confusion and sadness. It was silly how distraught she seemed about them not being in love. "No one. I just saw the way you looked at each other, felt the sparks and the level of comfort and trust between you. It was all ideal and racing toward a happy ending in my mind." She pursed her lips. "I'm sorry. I hope I haven't embarrassed you. My husband is the best but very solemn, and sometimes he says I am far too open and living in a fairy tale world." She winked. "It's a good place to live."

Esther forced a smile. This woman was genuine, and Esther liked her. The problem was, she was spot on. Reed was perfect to her, and she loved the sparks, the comfort, the way he looked at her, and even the trust. How was she going to stay strong? Especially alone in a romantic spa? She wanted to follow her brother's advice and not think about the future and just enjoy tonight, but she feared if she did that, she'd fall head over heels for Reed.

If Roman couldn't handle her clinginess and obsession with him, and he was a bit pompous and had loved her attention until he hadn't, how would a tough, independent, alpha male, hot sheriff respond?

She shuddered. She didn't want to find out.

Chapter Eight

Esther walked out of the women's locker room behind Kari and glanced around the gorgeous space. It was softly lit and she could see several pools. One was a small square, another a slightly larger square with what looked like wooden-slat beds in it, and the last pool was huge and rectangular with different waterspouts placed around it and a rock waterfall at the far end. Next to the pools were tile beds that didn't look too appetizing as well as comfortable-looking lay down beds and a bar with a variety of drinks in glass containers and a glass container with cookies in it.

She could hardly wait to use all the jets in the huge pool. She absolutely loved hydrotherapy and how soothing and relaxing this beautiful spot was.

Her gaze moved to the entrance to the men's locker room where one Sheriff Reed Peterson stepped out of the shadows. Her mouth gaped open, and her gaze traveled over his fit body without her fully giving herself permission to ogle him like that. She'd seen how his shirt had clung to the muscles of his chest and shoulders when he'd gotten soaked in the waterfall with her, but seeing the smooth muscle and skin uncovered was a bit much for the faint of heart. And she definitely felt faint of heart at the moment.

She stared at how well-formed and honestly beautiful he was, and then she finally met his gaze. His dark eyes were full of hope. He knew he looked good, but he wasn't cocky about it. He only hoped it was a point in his favor. It was more than a point. She longed to be held close against his beautiful shape.

Closing her eyes, she said a prayer for strength and forgiveness. She wouldn't want someone gaping over her in a swimsuit. Besides, Reed's insides were much more important and impressive than his outsides.

Luckily, Kari was talking and Esther could focus on her and not the way she'd gaped at Reed.

"So you start in the steam room. I'll give you chilled cloths to cover your eyes and noses and set the timer for twenty minutes. When you come out, your fairy godmother will have disappeared." She placed her hand on her chest and laughed.

Esther and Reed both smiled at her. Despite the embarrassing things she'd said, she was adorable and impossible not to like. Esther wanted to ask for no steam room. She didn't like them.

"Then you jump in the cold plunge."

"Cold plunge?" Esther asked. "I got enough of the cold water at the waterfall Saturday." She gave Reed a wink.

He grinned. "You were very brave."

"Ah, thank you, sweetheart."

Kari grinned. "I'm definitely writing a waterfall into your story. I promise the cold plunge feels awesome after being so hot in the steam room. Plus, the steam room opens your pores and then the cold plunge closes them up and invigorates you."

"We'll take your word for it," Esther said, but she gritted her teeth. She'd loved the hydrotherapy she'd done in Cancun with different pools and water jets to soothe every sore muscle, but she hadn't enjoyed the steam room or lasted more than a few minutes before she had to escape. She'd felt trapped and out of control. Hopefully she wouldn't flip out today and scare Reed away.

"Good. Then you go to the larger pool and play around with all the jets for as long as you want. There is a jet for every part of your body," Kari explained.

Esther nodded. That had been her favorite part of hydrotherapy. Using the jets as long as she wanted on different sore or tight muscles.

"Then you go to the bubble pool," Kari continued. "There's a button on the side of the pool to turn the bubbles on. Just relax and enjoy. When you're sick of the water, you can lie on the heated tile beds and the other recliners as long as you want, eat cookies and drink juice and do ... whatever you want." She winked as if whatever they wanted was to kiss for a long, long time. Esther's body got far too warm. "Or you can go back in the water. Gavin and I absolutely love kissing in the water."

Esther's face was surely beet red. She didn't look at Reed.

Kari wasn't done. "Or you can simply hold each other as you are weightless in the water and the cares of the world float away on barely perceptible ripples. Or ..." She grinned. "You can look into each other's eyes, gaze upon the soul while it's so open and accessible with no stress and nothing but each other to focus on."

Esther almost laughed at this author setting the scene for them, but she was too embarrassed. She glance askance at Reed. He gave her a confident and appealing smile. Kari's words didn't bother him, and he was man enough to hold Esther or let her "gaze upon his soul." She couldn't help but smile at him. He was even more impressive to take this level of teasing or embarrassment or whatever this was.

Kari was beaming at them. "Whatever you two prefer." She clapped her hands together. "What am I forgetting? Oh, there are towels by the bar. Reed, do you want a robe and slippers?"

"No." It sounded like he was laughing, as if a tough man wouldn't wear a robe.

Esther laughed too, appreciating the break in the romantic tension Kari had created.

"I see. Smart man. Use that fine-looking body to your advantage."

Esther laughed harder, and Reed actually looked chagrined. He might be the one blushing now.

Kari clapped her hands together. "All right. Let's steam all the stress and impurities out of you." She walked to a small fridge by the steam room and took out a tray of rolled wash cloths. They both walked to her. Using tongs, she lifted a cloth to each of them. It was chilled and almost too cold against Esther's fingers. "You're welcome to more of these whenever you want them. In you go."

She opened the door and steam poured out. It smelled delicious, like mint and eucalyptus.

"Take off that robe," Kari exclaimed, grabbing at Esther's robe.

Esther untied the straps and Kari slid it off her shoulders. She didn't dare look at Reed to see if he was staring at her like she'd stared at him in his swimsuit. She worked out hard every day, but she didn't have some perfect body.

Reed stepped up close and his hand rested on her lower back. His palm on her bare skin was a tantalizing feeling. Warmth flushed through Esther, and she didn't think she needed any time in that hot steam room to want to jump in the cold plunge and bring her core temperature down.

"You look amazing," he whispered in her ear.

She whipped around to look at him. "Oh, honey, you have no clue how amazing you look."

He grinned.

Kari laughed and shooed them with her hands. "Get on in there. You're losing all the good steam."

Reed smiled and escorted her in. Esther hoped they had lost some of the steam. The suffocating, choking steam.

The door shut behind them and though there were lights through the fog of steam, Esther could not see a single thing. Her eyes instantly stung, and breathing was difficult with the dense air. She just had to get through this part and then the beautiful part of the water and the jets and the actual relaxation could begin. She knew it would be even more fun and relaxing with Reed next to her.

"I don't think we lost any steam," she sputtered, but then she started coughing on the moisture in the air.

Reed lifted her hand with the washcloth gripped in it to her face. She got the hint and quickly unrolled it and put it over her eyes, nose, and mouth. Breathing in through the coolness of the cloth helped a lot. He slowly escorted her forward. They bumped into a bench, turned, and sat down.

The door flung open and luckily some steam escaped. "I forgot towels!" Kari cried out. "My heavens, you two are so sparkly and perfect that all I can think about is writing it all down." She rushed in and handed over two bath towels, then ran back out again. "It's comfier sitting on those. Hugs and much happiness to you both!"

The door shut, and she was gone.

Esther and Reed stood and sat on the soft towels. It was nice not to sit on the hot, steamy tile, but the steam they'd lost when Kari entered rose quickly again. It was certainly an efficient steam room.

"Do you think we'll get royalties from whatever story she writes about us?" Esther asked.

Reed laughed. "She's a little crazy."

"Aren't we all?" She felt stung by Reed thinking Kari was crazy. If only he knew who he was sitting next to. "I like her."

"For sure. She's friendly and welcoming. She's impossible not to like, and still a little crazy."

Esther took slow, shallow breaths. She didn't want to talk about crazy anymore. "Did she really say twenty minutes in here?"

Reed chuckled, not seeming as affected by the steam as she was. "If we want our pores and our nasal passages cleaned out."

"Mission accomplished. At least it smells good."

He laughed again.

"I don't think I'm cleaned out or exfoliated, but I'm already baked clear through."

"Steamed, I think," Reed said, laughter in his voice.

Sweat poured from her, or maybe it was steam. Who knew? She probably should stop complaining, but Reed seemed to think it was funny. He was such a chill, nice guy. But was he afraid of crazy? Not that it mattered. This was their last date.

In the moment, she reminded herself.

Their arms rubbed against each other, and the steam room got even warmer. She was panting for oxygen. Was that because of Reed's firm, muscular arm brushing hers or the fact she couldn't draw a full breath without coughing on the moisture?

She tried to regulate her breathing and her heartbeat, but she couldn't calm down and feared she might be headed toward a panic attack. She hadn't had one in a long, long time. This was the worst possible moment for it to happen again.

Still unable to see through the steam, she wanted to turn to Reed, bury her head in his firm chest, and see if he could help her calm down. No, that was the absolute wrong idea. Clinging to Reed's perfect body would make her more out of breath, and her pulse would skyrocket.

There was only one solution. Unless Reed really wanted to see a version of crazy out of the usually calm lawyer that put Kari to shame, she had to get out of here. Now.

She stood, gripping her washcloth to her eyes and managed, "I can't take it."

"Okay," Reed said calmly.

Esther tried to walk to the door, but she ran into a wall. She was out of control and out of her element. She started to hyperventilate, sucking in more water-filled air and coughing on the exhale. If she didn't get dry air soon, she was going to pass out. Everything was out of control. She hated out of control.

A warm arm came around her waist and Reed pulled her in tight to his side. The world stabilized. She might just survive this. He escorted her across the steam room, pushed open the door, and they stepped out into dry, normal air.

Reed held her close as she pulled in quick breaths. Her coughing settled and her heart, lungs, and head didn't feel ready to burst.

"It's okay," he murmured. "You're okay, slow and easy. In ..."

She pulled in a breath.

"And out."

She pushed it all out.

Esther felt her lungs calming down, though her body was still sweaty and hot. Reed close by and being so reasonable was calming her down from the panic of being stuck in that steam room.

Reed close by was also heating her up and making her heart race from his beautiful nearness.

He talked her through some more slow breaths and then looked her over. "Better?"

She nodded. She *was* better. He was like her calm in the midst of the storm. If only she could cling to him whenever she flipped out. She didn't flip out very often. Usually with prayer and escaping the situation when needed, she made it through with no one being the wiser.

Suddenly she was humiliated. Reed had seen her freak out. He wasn't looking at her like she was nuts, but he probably hid his emotions often as the sheriff.

"Sorry," she murmured, looking down. "I didn't mean to freak out like that. I couldn't breathe and was coughing."

"No worries. I'm with you. It felt like I was suffocating in there."

"Me too." She debated apologizing or explaining more, but at the waterfall she'd begged him not to ask about her issues and he'd said he wouldn't. No reason to make him wonder more now. Especially after Kari's gazing into the soul instructions.

She appreciated how kind he was being and that he had stabilized and strengthened her. But it seemed even more important to keep hiding what was really going on in her head. This impressive man could not know she was crazy.

"Cold plunge?" she redirected.

"I thought you'd never ask." He grinned and extended his hand.

Esther only hesitated briefly before putting her hand in his. She had to somehow take Thor's advice and keep having fun. Reed hadn't called her nuts for her panicked reaction to the steam room. She loved him for that, or she should think *appreciated* him for that. She shouldn't make a big deal out of it if he wasn't.

They hurried across the tiled floor to the nearby cold plunge. Two steps in, with bitter cold swirling around her ankles, she was already doubting she wanted to go under.

"Together?" Reed asked.

"Okay." She took a deep breath and jumped forward to clear the rest of the steps.

They plunged off the steps and into the ice-cold water. Esther forced herself to go under completely. She burst up out of the water and Reed was right there.

He grinned, wiping the water off his face and making it impossible to not notice how his biceps and shoulder muscles flexed with that move. "Whew! That feels awesome. Maybe the misery of the steam room was worth the cold plunge."

"Did you really think the steam room was suffocating and miserable too?" she asked. Was he only trying to commiserate?

He nodded. His dark eyes were clear and guileless. Reed had nothing to hide. If only she could say the same. "I was starting to wonder what you loved about this hydrotherapy."

She grinned and tugged on his hand. "Come on, sweetie, and I'll show you."

"Lead the way, beautiful."

Esther doubted she looked beautiful. She was probably bright red from the heat of the steam room and the sting of the cold pool, and her makeup was probably smeared down her face. Reed didn't seem to care.

She led him over to the large pool and they took their time trying out each of the different jets that massaged every stiff and tired muscle from their bottom of their feet to the crowns of their heads. It felt every bit as good as she remembered.

They went back to the neck and upper back jets and stayed there for a while. Then she took him to the bubble bed, and they floated as the bubbles relaxed them. Esther was so relaxed she probably would've fallen asleep. If she hadn't been next to the handsome and invigorating Reed Peterson. "Hot sheriff" was such an insufficient label for the kind, patient, fun, smart, and intriguing man. Kari's words kept going through her mind, and she wished they could hold each other while their worries floated away.

They finally looked like prunes and climbed out of the water. He wrapped a towel around his waist and she put the robe back on. They ate the delicious chocolate chip and snickerdoodle cookies and drank a few different teas and juices before settling on the pineapple juice as their favorite. They tried out the surprisingly comfortable and ergonomically correct tile beds for a while, then moved to the plush lay down beds. They started chatting about work and families and time flew by.

Esther wondered how late it was. Her skin felt tight, her hair frizzy, and her eyes were grainy, but she was loath to end the night. Would it be out of line to take Reed's hand, without any hesitation this time, tug him back into that warm pool, pull her hot sheriff in tight, and kiss him for a really, really long time?

Kari would definitely approve, but sadly it was probably wrong. Especially since Esther was planning on not going on another date with him.

Tonight had been perfect. The dream date that surpassed every other date she'd ever been on. Even the memories of the steam room were good because Reed had rescued, soothed, and strengthened her afterward.

But all good things had to come to an end. Garret wasn't a danger any longer and there was no reason to keep dating Reed ... Except for Reed.

He looked at her with those deep-brown eyes of his and for a moment she forgot every fear she had of getting into another relationship. Yet if Reed realized how crazy she got and dumped her ... It would hurt much, much worse than when Roman had. She hadn't let herself fall in love for over ten years, and she honestly didn't know if she could stop the downward spiral if she lost Reed. At least Reed wouldn't die because of her obsession.

At the same time, she'd acted pretty nuts at the waterfall, and again in the steam room, and he'd not only taken both in stride but he'd proven he was solid, steady, and wouldn't make her feel stupid if she had a moment of insanity.

"We'd better go," she said softly.

He nodded and stood, holding out his hand.

Esther stared at his lovely chest, shoulders, and arms. Her gaze made its way up to his handsome face. She knew and loved that face. How was she going to push him away after tonight? Could Papa come up with an assignment that got her away from the valley? She had the seniority and experience to request a move with the Air Force. That might take some time though, and she didn't know how she'd resist Reed any longer.

She put her hand in his. He smiled and gently lifted her off the plush bed. Instead of releasing her hand, he tugged her toward him. Esther's hands landed on his chest and his hands easily slid around her lower back.

A slow smile grew on his handsome face, and his dark eyes were full of her. He was gone over her. She could read that without being a romance novelist.

Warning bells should be clanging, but Esther pushed them away in the beauty of the moment and the romantic quiet of this place with the waterfall's soothing sound, the smell of mint and eucalyptus, the low lighting, but most importantly the incredible man leaning closer and closer to her.

She arched up and slid her hands across his chest and around his neck. Anticipation and warmth swirled around them better than even the warm water and relaxing jets of the therapy pool.

No words were needed as their lips softly met. The promise of passion, love, and safety lingered in his incredible kiss.

The men's locker room door burst open. They broke apart and turned to see a well-built, thirty-something guy with dark hair and eyes stride into the pool area. He saw them embracing and froze. "Ah, crap." He pushed a hand through his hair. "You're still here."

Esther released her grip on Reed, but he kept one arm around her.

"Sorry, man," Reed said. "We lost track of time. We'll go change and head out. I really appreciate you giving us a private booking."

"No," the man grunted out.

Esther wasn't sure what he was saying no to, but it was a forceful, desperate sounding no. He seemed like the type of guy who didn't talk much. He reminded her of her brother Greer, actually. Tough, loyal, and far too quiet. The only person who cajoled Greer into talking was his girlfriend Emery.

The guy put up both hands and pushed out a heavy breath. "Kari's going to beat me."

Esther laughed at that. Reed laughed with her, and this serious guy even smiled. No way was the angelic and verbose Kari going to beat her husband.

Some of the embarrassment of being caught kissing in front of this guy dissipated. Though the frustration of the unfulfilled kiss was strong, her head was clearing from the Reed-induced fog, a fog that was beautiful but made it hard to see clearly. She realized Kari's husband had helped her dodge a bullet. "Gavin Strong?" she asked.

"Guilty." He nodded. "Sorry. Thought the lights got left on." He shook his head. "Stay ... Please."

"We've been here long enough," Esther rushed out. "It's such a beautiful facility and your wife is a doll. She'll never hear from us that you came to ... check on the lights." Her neck heated up. She continued to take the focus away from him seeing them kissing. "As your legal counsel, if she does find out, I suggest you offer a plea bargain in exchange for kissing in the pools. She told us she loves that."

"Thanks," he grunted, clearly embarrassed at interrupting them, or maybe at her mentioning kissing in the pools.

Esther broke from Reed's grasp, not looking at him. She hated that their time here was done and hated that they'd been interrupted, but it was for the best. It was wrong of her to kiss Reed when she knew their dating time was done. She didn't want to take advantage of someone as incredible as Reed. It hurt to think of not being alone with him again. She'd loved every second of laughing, talking, and enjoying being with Reed, but she had to be unselfish and she had to get away. Now. Or she'd throw herself at him even with Gavin Strong watching on.

"I'll go change. Thank you again." She hurried toward the women's locker room. As she pushed through the door, she glanced back.

Reed's gaze was full of longing, and it made her heart give a weird hitch.

Esther Delta-Peterson. She didn't think she could go there, but it hurt to think of never being joined to an amazing man like Reed.

She kept claiming she had her OCD under control and it didn't control her life any longer, but ditching this amazing man rather than risk her OCD surfacing and messing her up again, and possibly hurting him, told her she couldn't win. Either the OCD controlled her if she let herself be swept into Reed's heart and arms and went insane, or the OCD controlled her because she missed out on any chance of being with Reed because of her fear. She hated either option and hated most of all that she'd been trained to be brave and protect herself physically, but she clearly didn't know how to succeed emotionally.

Chapter Nine

Reed thanked Gavin Strong again. The guy was clearly embarrassed that he'd interrupted their kiss, but he wasn't to blame. Reed should've kissed Esther twenty times before he actually accomplished it tonight, but he'd wanted to take things slow and not push or scare her.

Reed rinsed off in a shower and quickly got dressed. He looked at his cell phone. Ten-twenty. Kari had said to stay as long as they wanted, but the booking was only from seven to nine. Reed was the one who should be embarrassed for overstaying their welcome and taking advantage of the Strongs' generosity.

He wished their kiss hadn't been interrupted, but the date had been incredible and he had high hopes he could not only re-initiate the kiss as he walked her to Thor's door, but that she would agree to another date tomorrow night. He was going to push past her three-date barrier and work his way into boyfriend status with his dream woman. Soon.

He hurried out into the main area and checked his phone while he waited for Esther. He rarely went very long without checking it, though luckily his valley was fairly quiet and his deputies and staff competent.

Josh had left a message to call him. He didn't see Gavin or Esther, so he pushed the call back. "Hey," he greeted Josh. "Sorry it's late."

"No, I'm glad you called. I'm not sure where this is going to go, but my buddy Niles with Colorado Springs PD called me. He said something about the name Garret Thomson was bugging him. He had a friend with that name in high school who'd gone on to be a dentist, but he hadn't heard from Garret in a while; not since the guy graduated dental school."

Esther walked out of the locker room, her long hair wet and no makeup on but wearing her dress. She was so beautiful, but something in her blue eyes looked wary and not as warm as usual. It concerned him more than whatever story Josh had about another guy with Garret Thomson's same name.

"Hey, Josh, Esther is here. Can I call you back about this?"

"She probably needs to hear this too."

"Okay." He had a feeling this was going to change the nature of the date. "Just a second while we get in the truck and I can put it through the Bluetooth."

"Okay." Josh sounded impatient, which wasn't normal for him.

Reed smiled at Esther. "Josh has something to tell us about Garret."

Her eyebrows rose. Her blue eyes seemed wary. She was probably as sick of Garret as he was. The guy was just a loser and didn't seem to be any threat to the Delta secret. Reed wanted to put all his focus where it should be ... on Esther.

Shifting the phone to his left hand, he escorted her to the door and opened it. "I'm not sure if we should turn off the lights and lock up," he said.

Gavin walked out of an office to their right at that moment, as if he'd been waiting for them to leave. He lifted a hand.

"Thanks again," Reed said.

"Yes, thank you so much. Dinner, the hydrotherapy, your darling wife, and everything was amazing," Esther said.

"Thanks." Gavin nodded to them.

Reed held the door, and then they walked across the parking lot to his truck. There were other vehicles in the parking lot still, probably guests staying at the beautiful lodge. No wonder Gavin hadn't known they were still in the spa as they were parked by the lodge entrance.

He helped Esther into the truck and then walked around. Loading up, he clicked on the speaker button on the phone and selected the Bluetooth option. "Okay, Josh. You've got us both."

"Hi, Esther."

"Hi, Josh." Esther clutched her hands together in her lap. Reed wasn't sure if she was nervous about the news or trying to keep from holding his hand. He didn't know why he'd even thought that. He didn't lack confidence around women he dated, but this was Esther. He wanted everything to be perfect with her, to keep dating her, and it was hard not to think that the older, accomplished, and gorgeous lawyer and Delta-trained fighter was out of his league.

Reed backed out of the stall and then dropped it into drive and drove away from their beautiful evening together.

Josh started talking immediately. "So I was telling Reed that my buddy Niles from the Colorado Springs Police Department was thinking how he had a friend named Garret Thomson he knew from back home in North Carolina. The guy went to dental school in Chicago, but after he graduated nobody heard from him again. Niles thought it was an odd coincidence they were both dentists and both spelled their name the same. So he went digging for info." He paused for breath. "Here's where it gets weird."

Reed glanced at Esther. In the glow of the dash lights, she looked even more unsteady.

"And?" he encouraged Josh.

"His Garret Thomson is gone, and he says the Garret Thomson who is a dentist in Colorado Springs now is *not* the same guy."

"Gone? What do you mean?" There could be two dentists with the name Garret Thomson.

"Apparently Garret's parents had passed while he was in undergrad and he didn't have much other family besides a sister. None of the friends back home have heard from Garret since he graduated dental school and when Niles called the sister earlier tonight to see if he could get Garret's current phone number, she said her brother had turned into a snob and told her he was a respectable dentist and not trailer trash any more so she shouldn't expect to ever see him again. She said he didn't even have the decency to call and dump his family. He sent it all in a text and then never responded to her calls or texts again."

Reed's neck tingled. He reached over and put his hand over Esther's clasped ones. She didn't hold his hand, but she didn't move hers away.

"So my friend's buddy Garret Thomson graduates from University of Illinois at Chicago School of Dentistry," Josh rushed on, "and then he accepts a job working with an older dentist in Colorado Springs. A Dr. James Olson. The same Dr. Olson that Esther's Garret Thomson worked with."

"So they're the same person?" Reed asked.

"I don't think so. Let me keep going and you decide. So Dr. Olson dies of a drug overdose a couple years later."

Reed's stomach tightened. He upped his speed as they left the quiet valley of Lone Peak and entered the canyon. Esther turned her hand over and their palms aligned. He held on to her hand and felt some of the stress lighten.

"It's not an uncommon thing, especially with the stress load of a dental practice, and the guy's wife had just divorced him. Dentists have a higher rate of suicide than any profession. But given that Niles and I both believe that the Garret Thomson Esther dated, and are all creeped out by, may have killed and stolen the other Garret Thomson's name, schooling, and accreditation, Dr. Olson's death is a little … unsettling."

"Unsettling? That escalated quickly. You think the Garret who was after Esther stole someone else's identity, that he isn't the Garret your buddy knew back in North Carolina? If that's true, it's horrifying. But could it be true?" Reed looked to Esther. She only shrugged. He had no love lost for the guy who'd semi-stalked Esther, but he'd seemed kind of shy and nerdy, not a killer. Could he really have stolen someone else's name, degree, and life, and then killed the dentist he worked for so he could take over his clients? How did the guy fake dental school training and have a successful practice?

"Well. The photos of Garret Thomson in high school, college, and dental school bear a similarity to our Garret Thomson, but he either had plastic surgery done after dental school or he is not the same guy."

Reed looked at Esther. "What do you think?"

"It's pretty crazy. Garret just told me he was from Chicago, but that doesn't make sense if he's really from North Carolina."

"Unless he doesn't want anybody checking with people who knew him in North Carolina." Reed thought this seemed pretty far-fetched, but Josh had already done a lot of research and he wanted to check every angle and make sure Esther was safe.

"I'll get Papa to look into it with his channels," Esther said.

He squeezed her hand. "That'll be good. Josh, can you see what you can find out from Chicago PD? Maybe a body that they couldn't identify close to Garret's age at the time he finished dental school or a violent crime they never solved and a reason a guy would kill someone to steal his identity? Circulate the photos of both Garret Thomsons and see if anything comes up."

"Sure thing." Josh sounded excited about the possibility of solving a violent crime, or possibly creating drama that wasn't there. "Chat soon."

The line went dead. Reed cleared the valley and headed south toward home. "What are you thinking?" he asked into the silence, gently stroking the back of Esther's soft hand with his thumb.

"It's a pretty good stretch, but worth looking into." She pursed her lips. "He gave me a free cleaning, X-rays, and filled a cavity for me. I thought he was a good dentist."

"It seems like the years of training to be a dentist would be impossible to fake." Which made him think there wasn't any credence to this story.

"Exactly." She was quiet for a second, then said, "I'd better call Papa."

"Oh. Okay."

She pulled her hand free and her phone out of her purse. He listened to her side of the conversation, which went on for a long time. He didn't want to be selfish, but he wanted to talk to Esther himself, philosophize and theorize on whether Garret Thomson might truly be a violent criminal and an imposter. He loved talking to her and getting her insights on anything and everything, and this story was definitely intriguing and worth debating.

She hung up as they were pulling into Summit Valley. Letting out a soft breath, she leaned her head against the seat cushion and looked at him. "Is it pathetic that I'm exhausted?"

"No. This is all a lot to take in."

"Emotionally draining for sure," she murmured, and he feared she wasn't only talking about the situation with Garret. Reed didn't want to emotionally drain her. He wanted to inspire, uplift, and restore her. He was being idealistic and selfish. He needed to focus on the Garret Thomson situation, not his desperate need to woo the beautiful Esther Delta. "Did Papa find anything?"

"Not yet, but he will."

"Should we be monitoring the guy's activities?" he asked.

"Papa had somebody check while we were talking."

"Papa Delta's connections are incredible."

She nodded. "A lot of military people owe him favors, so finding someone in Colorado Springs so close to the Air Force base was probably easy. Anyway, they confirmed with neighbors that Garret got home from work tonight about six-thirty and hasn't left. There was a heat signature inside in the kitchen. They'll make sure he doesn't leave tonight and tomorrow assign a tail to him until we can clear him of any wrongdoing with the other Garret Thomson."

"Okay." Could he reach for her hand again? They drove to the east and up the canyon that led to the Deltas' homes. Why did he feel like his time with her was expiring?

"Neither of us can think of any reason this would relate to the Delta secret," she said. "So that's good news."

She sounded exhausted.

"For sure. We've had enough crazies going after that lately. No need to add one more psycho to the stack."

Her brow squiggled, and she studied him for a second before saying, "I'm so grateful nobody in our family has been hurt yet. Hopefully Papa gets to the bottom of who's sending men after the secret soon."

Reed nodded.

"I hate that I'm putting more burden on him. It was annoying that Garret kept texting, calling, and leaving me stuff after the three dates and then shadowing me a few days ago, but he's never acted violent."

"We still need to get to the bottom of it. I'll keep you safe." He tried to say it all serious and meaningful, but they were still driving and he couldn't touch her while he said it or look deeply into her eyes, so he was afraid it lost some of its potency.

Esther said nothing, which worried him. They stopped in front of Thor's house and he pulled on his door handle.

"Wait," Esther said. "I need to tell you something."

Reed released his door and glanced across the console. He knew she was tired, but he wanted to walk her to the door and hold her close for at least a minute. He could wait on the kiss, but he needed her in his arms. Maybe he could walk her inside and hold her until she fell asleep and then carry her up to her room and tuck her in. His blood heated up. He doubted Thor would approve of that plan, though, even if he and Reed were close friends.

"Sure. Anything." He made his voice upbeat even though it wobbled slightly.

Esther worried her lip, then spit out, "Reed, you're an incredible guy and I appreciate you being so trustworthy and loyal, helping my family so much with the Delta secret, and doing this fake date situation with me, but I think we're ... past all of that."

"Past all of ... what?"

"Fake dating." She drew in a breath. "Dating."

Reed's stomach flipped, and he shook his head. "Esther, I told you this was never fake for me."

She looked straight into his eyes, and he could see how serious she was in the dim light from the dash. "I really appreciate you, Reed. You're an incredible and kind man." She swallowed, then said forcibly, "It was all fake for me." She yanked on her door handle and literally jumped out of his truck. "We'll keep in touch on the Garret situation. Thanks for all the help. Night!"

She slammed the truck door, ran around the front of his truck and up to the front porch. Within seconds, she'd disappeared inside.

Reed didn't even move. He didn't try to stop her, chase after her, declare his love and beg her to make it real, to feel something for him.

His heart thudded dully in his chest. He was surprised it kept beating at all. *It was all fake for me. It was all fake for me.* Her words played over and over in his head.

How could Esther, the woman he adored, have said those harsh, awful words in such an unemotional, level tone as she looked into his eyes? He wanted to convince himself she was lying to protect her heart, or his, or maybe something with the Delta secret. He'd heard scattered talk about one of the grandchildren being made Secret Keeper. Maybe Esther had been appointed and thought she couldn't focus on dating and love until they found whoever was sending people after the secret?

He banged his head against the steering wheel. He hated the excuses. Esther didn't want him. It was plain and simple, and he'd better get used to it.

What had happened to the warm, fun, beautiful, smart woman he'd taken on three incredible dates? Well, she was still fun, beautiful, and smart, but definitely not warm. Not when she told him it was all fake for her.

She'd willingly kissed him tonight before Gavin Strong had interrupted. Had she just let her guard down, then remembered she didn't want him later?

Thor had warned him. Three dates and done. Was that how she'd dumped the other men? How many? Hundreds? He could only imagine how many men pursued Esther and she kindly said yes, called them *sweetie* and *honey* and was adorable and warm ... until date number three was over.

Was his dream woman really a cold heartbreaker?

It was a long, long time until he lifted his head and put the truck in gear. He needed to focus on Garret Thomson and what was happening there. Garret showing up at the restaurant still bugged him. What if the guy was still tracking her and he was bad news?

Reed had to focus and keep her safe, but all he could think about was Esther ditching him. Nothing had ripped him apart this bad since his dad had died.

Chapter Ten

Esther's entire body shook from the emotion of lying to the love of her life. Somehow, she made it in through the front door and up the steps. Thor called to her from the main area, but she dashed to her bedroom without responding. She couldn't.

Once her bedroom door was safely closed behind her, she allowed the tears to come. She wanted to fall onto the bed and cry herself to sleep, but something pulled her to the window. Reed's truck sat there. Why didn't he drive away?

What if he came after her?

A thrill raced through her, but she quickly shoved it away. How long could she keep lying to him? She should receive some sort of actress award for pulling it off tonight like she had. She'd kept a straight face and hopefully had kept the longing for him out of her eyes as she'd said it was all fake for her.

She should be worried about the whole weird deal with Garret Thomson or what she needed to do for the Delta secret if Garret was somehow a threat, but all she could manage to do was let the tears silently trail down her face and pray Reed wouldn't hate her. That he would know it wasn't him; it really was her. He was incredible. He was everything she'd ever want. But she couldn't do it. If she'd been obsessed with Roman, she would be fanatically psychotic about Reed. With Garret possibly being a killer, it hit her that she'd brought that to Reed's doorstep. If something happened to Reed because of her, she wouldn't survive.

Should she have told him the real truth? That she was crazy? Psychotic? He'd said those words a few times around her. He'd definitely stay away if she admitted what was really happening in her head, but she selfishly didn't want him or anyone else to know.

A soft rap came at the door. She couldn't respond. She prayed it was Reed and then she prayed it wasn't. Why couldn't she give him a chance, see if the way he'd calmed her down at the waterfall, tenderly putting her socks on and being so steady and awesome when she'd grabbed his shirt and demanded he not ask any questions, or the way he'd calmed her down after the steam room and acted like it was no big deal, were reminiscent of how he could be there for her if her OCD reared its ugly head.

But what if he called her crazy or psychotic? She'd really fall apart.

What if Garret came after Reed because Esther had selfishly gone out with him? Garret may seem like a wimp compared to Reed, but if Josh's story proved true, he was an unstable murderer.

The door cracked open. "Sis?"

Thor. That was good.

She swallowed hard and turned from staring at Reed's truck, which still hadn't moved, and hoped Thor couldn't see her tears in the dark room. "Hey, bro. Did you hear about Garret? Psychotic, right?" She winced at using that word.

"For sure." Thor pushed the door wider. He walked to her side and looked at her and then down at Reed's truck. Still not moving. "Is that why you're crying and why Reed isn't pulling away?"

Esther swallowed hard again, but she couldn't clear the tightness or emotion from her throat. "I guess. I'm exhausted and overwrought. What a day. Is Shell here?"

"I took her home a couple hours ago, but I waited up for you."

"Ah, such a good brother." Her voice trembled with emotion.

"Esther ..." He looked her over and to her horror, more tears leaked out. "You are not okay. Is this about Garret or about Reed?"

At the sound of Reed's name, she cried harder.

Thor wrapped an arm around her and drew her in tight. "Ah, sis. What happened?"

She couldn't stop the torrent of tears from releasing. She couldn't explain. Thor wouldn't understand. Maybe Papa, Dad, or Mom would understand, but sometimes she didn't think they truly got it either. How could anybody who hadn't been where she'd been truly comprehend why she had to keep her distance from romantic relationships and love?

Her rule had failed her this time. It was too late.

She already loved Reed.

"Three dates and done?" Thor guessed.

Esther nodded against his shoulder.

"I'm not gonna lie, it ticks me off that you'd do that to my boy."

Esther half-laughed at that. "Then be ticked off. I do it to everybody."

"But why, sis?" Thor pulled back slightly and looked into her eyes. "I guess it's an okay policy if you're dating losers, or even to see if the guy is cool before pursuing more with him, but Reed is the biggest stud we know. How could you date and dump him?"

"I never should've dated him," she admitted.

"That's a stupid excuse. You two are perfect together."

"I'm not perfect."

"Esther." Thor's voice was full of warning. "You're the most incredible sister in the world and the only woman more perfect than you is Shelly, and maybe Mama."

That made her laugh again, but 'perfect' was almost as big of a trigger for her as 'crazy.' "I've got to sleep," she said. "Too much emotion, and the deal with Garret, and ... I'll process better in the morning."

Thor studied her and lifted a warning finger. "In the morning, after I do chores, I expect your Swedish pancakes, well-done bacon, and a fruit parfait ready, then you're going to spill your guts to me."

Esther laughed. Her brothers loved to demand she cook for them. "I'll cook for you because I love you and I'm staying at your house, but I'm not burning the bacon. And I'll decide about the spilling of guts." No way. If she couldn't be brave enough to tell Reed about her messed-up emotional health, no way was she spilling it to her brother.

"Okay. Just not limp bacon, please."

"You got it."

He gave her one more hug and then walked to the door. "I love you, sis. Get some rest. Everything will look better in the morning."

Esther forced a smile. "For sure. Thanks, Thor. I love you."

He lifted a hand and closed the door behind him.

Esther's gaze darted to the window. Reed's truck was gone. The tears started afresh.

She quickly washed her face, brushed her teeth, slid into a tank top and shorts, prayed, and climbed into bed. Stretching out on the soft sheets felt incredible, but she couldn't sleep. She'd thought she was exhausted, but now a restless energy and the stress of everything rotating through her brain kept her up.

She paced some laps around the room, but it felt stuffy and confining. She opened the window, but even that much fresh air wasn't enough. Creeping out of the room and down the stairs, she went through the great room and out the back patio door. The night was crisp as only a summer night in the high mountains could be. It felt incredible and refreshing and cleared her mind a little.

She wandered around Thor's yard, the grass cool and damp against her bare feet. No ideas or heavenly inspiration came to her, but she felt more calm as she looked up through the pine trees at the deep blue sky studded with stars. The world was so big and the universe even more so, but she knew her Heavenly Father still watched over and cared about her. It blew her mind, but she knew it was true.

Please help me not hurt Reed, she prayed.

After pacing for a while, she finally got tired. She lay down on one of the squishy patio couches and stretched out, closing her eyes. Drifting in and out, she was comfortable and exhausted and ...

Were those footsteps? And heavy breathing?

She tried to open her eyes, but her lids felt like they weighed a thousand pounds. She had to be imagining the sounds anyway and wasn't certain if she was awake or asleep and dreaming.

Hot breath brushed across her neck and then hands wrapped around her neck. A vise grip cut off her air supply.

Esther's eyes flew open. She gasped for oxygen that wasn't available and tried to pry the strong hands away from her throat as she looked into the steely blue gaze of Garret Thomson.

He smiled coldly at her as she dug her fingernails into his hands and flailed to get free. "If I can't have you, the county sheriff can't," he sneered. "I'll kill him after I kill you."

Anger filled her. This guy truly was psychotic. She refused to die at his hands and she certainly wouldn't allow him to hurt Reed.

She forced her mind to calm even as it screamed for oxygen and escape from his bruising fingers. She was strong and although Garret had a stronger grip than she would've imagined, he would not control her. She drew on years of training and visualized what Papa would have her do.

Releasing her grip on Garret's fingers, she jabbed an elbow hard into his forearm and at the same time brought her knee up and kneed him in the side of his abdomen. His breath rushed out and his hands relaxed slightly.

It was enough. She jammed her finger into his eye.

He squealed and yanked away, covering his eye and screaming like a baby.

Esther drew in a ragged breath. The sweet air burned her throat and her raw lungs. Still, the fight was far from over. She sat up and punched him in the same eye that his hand was covering.

He flew back on the couch, screaming louder still and cursing repeatedly.

Lights flipped on inside. Esther was still trying to get enough oxygen in and somehow calm her burning lungs and throat. Thankfully she'd had enough strength, probably fueled by the sheer will to live, to fight him off until Thor came.

Garret scrambled away from her and ran.

"No," Esther croaked out. No way could that jerk get away.

She pushed off the couch and stood shakily, pursuing him on trembling legs. The adrenaline she'd had to fight him must have dissipated and the weakness from nearly being strangled was far too evident as he widened his lead.

Garret disappeared into the forest behind Thor's house.

Esther kept pushing forward. She reached the edge of the forest as the back door flung open.

"Esther!" Thor hollered.

She ran off the soft grass and into the forest, branches and rocks and pinecones poking at her bare feet. She had no idea where to go. It was dark and her head throbbed from lack of oxygen.

Thor reached her, grabbing her arm. "What happened? Are you okay?"

"Garret," she choked out, pointing at her throat. "Tried to ... kill me."

"No," her brother growled. His eyes flashed a darker blue and he took off through the forest. He was in only a pair of shorts, no shoes or a flashlight. Esther wanted to call to him, but no way could she croak out a yell. Thor would pursue whether it was smart or not.

She turned and headed back for the house. The best route was calling her dad, Papa, and ... Sheriff Reed. Her heart hurt at even the thought of his name, but Reed would help them find and apprehend Garret. More importantly, she had to warn him that Garret could be after him.

A motor roared to life and then gunned off down the road. Crap. He must've skimmed the forest and headed for his car. She rushed toward the house, but knew she'd be too late to chase him in her Cherokee or Thor's truck. By the time she called and got anybody out of bed, they wouldn't find him. Maybe Reed or his deputies had a chance; Garret had to get down the canyon and through Summit Valley before escaping. Hopefully he was still driving a Mustang.

She rushed through the house and up the stairs, her limbs heavy and her throat raw. She stumbled into her bedroom and ripped her phone off the dresser. Pushing Reed's number on the recent calls made her shiver. If only she were calling for a different reason.

It rang three times and then the husky and wonderful voice of her hot sheriff came on the line. "Esther?"

Esther bit her lip. His sleepy voice was so appealing. She hated that she'd had to ditch him. Garret coming after her, and threatening Reed, was another testimony. Garret would hurt Reed if he could, and it would be on her head.

"I ... need you," she managed.

"Ah, love, I need you too," he said so quickly it robbed her of the oxygen she was still trying to get back to her bloodstream.

"Oh, Reed." Her voice was scratchy and painful. "Not like that. Garret tried to kill me."

"Esther!" His voice was full of horror. "Where is he? I'll rip him apart."

Esther almost smiled at the protective tone in his voice. "Just left Thor's place, heading toward Summit Valley. He has a red Ford Mustang. He threatened to kill you too."

"Let him try." Reed laughed like that was a joke. If only it was. How could she make sure he stayed safe? "You're okay, love?"

Esther knew he needed to hang up and dispatch his deputies, but he was concerned for her. That touched her heart. "Yes," she said as calmly and convincingly as she could.

"I've got to go. I'll come check on you soon." The call disconnected.

"Be ... careful." He was already gone. Esther held it to her heart and wished she could love him, could let him love her.

She allowed herself three seconds of longing, then she set her jaw and focused. The next number she dialed was Papa's.

Chapter Eleven

Reed spent an exhausting night searching Summit Valley and the surrounding canyons and roads, corresponding with law enforcement throughout Colorado to find Garret Thomson and a red Mustang or black Jeep truck, the vehicles he had registered in his name.

Of course, the Delta family was combing the area as well and Papa Delta was putting all his connections to work. Reed wouldn't be surprised if an elite military squad had been dispatched.

They came up with nothing. It was frustrating. Reed wanted that man behind bars, then he could comfort and love Esther.

If she'd let him.

By morning, nothing had changed except the eerie news that Josh had done a bang-up job with his research. He'd worked with Papa Delta's contacts and the dental school in Chicago and together they'd pieced together a chilling story.

Robert Bend, a quiet and brilliant kid from Cleveland, Ohio, had been a model dental school student at the University of Illinois Chicago School of Dentistry. He'd fallen in love with another student, Mary Fontaine. She'd broken up with him at the end of their final year, right before their summative exams. Her friends said he was acting crazily obsessed with her and she'd needed a break so she could focus on the final exams and have some space from him.

Mary had turned up missing the night before the exams. Robert had completed his exams with stellar performances on written and in-person testing. Three days later, Mary's body had been found. She'd been choked to death and put in Lake Michigan with a brick tied to her foot, but some fisherman had pulled her up. They never found Robert for questioning. He disappeared off the map.

At about the same time, Garret Thomson, Robert's roommate coincidentally, got a great job offer with an older dentist, Dr. James Olson, and moved to Colorado Springs for work. Josh was one hundred percent convinced Robert had killed Garret too, but had been smarter about hiding the body, had gotten plastic surgery to change his appearance to be similar to Garret's, and had assumed his old roommate's identity before Garret's first day of work in Colorado Springs.

When Robert's family was questioned, they said he sent texts regularly and called occasionally, but he hadn't been home even for Christmas since he finished dental school.

It was sickening, and Reed could hardly stand to think of Esther ever being close to such a depraved lunatic. Garret must've gotten obsessed with Esther as well. Thankfully, she hadn't been his next victim. The police were looking into some unsolved cases of women close to Garret or Robert's age in the various locations he'd lived to see if they'd ever had an association with him. So far, they had seven possibilities from Ohio, Chicago, and Colorado Springs.

By noon, Reed was exhausted. He still hadn't made it up to the Deltas' valley to see Esther and still hadn't found a lead on Garret.

At four, they got a call from Lonepeak Valley's sheriff's department. They'd been scouring their valley, especially as Reed and Esther had been there last night and they wondered if Garret had somehow followed them. They'd found the red Ford Mustang registered to Garret Thomson when they realized an elderly couple's Buick had disappeared from their detached garage. The couple rarely drove but were proud that they kept the gas tank full and the keys in the car in case any of their family or caretakers needed a vehicle. They'd searched further and found the Mustang hidden in the barn under some tarps and old blankets.

So now they were looking for a silver Buick Lucerne, and everyone philosophized that Garret had probably switched cars before he attacked Esther. They'd been looking for the wrong vehicle the entire time. Garret had probably secured a different vehicle by now or was already hidden somewhere. As smart as Garret was, and as many crimes as he'd committed, he probably had several IDs in his possession.

Reed loathed the thought of this being an unsolved crime. It was very, very personal to him.

He sat at his desk and suddenly he could hear Esther's voice late last night, raspy because she'd almost been choked to death.

I... need you.

His heart had about launched from his chest and he'd been instantly awake. He'd responded that he needed her, too.

Not like that.

That line had hurt almost as much as her saying it was all fake. Esther was good at ripping his heart out, but he refused to walk away from her. He'd do everything in his power to keep her safe and somehow help her be happy. Even if it wasn't happiness with him.

His heart gave a painful twist at Esther being with anyone else.

His phone rang, and he snatched up the excuse to stop thinking so much. "Papa," he greeted Esther's grandfather.

"You heard they found the Mustang?"

"Yes, sir. I'm thinking I'll go start searching for that Buick." He didn't know what else to do at this point.

"There are plenty of police officers, FBI, and military searching for Garret Thomson and that Buick, though he's likely changed cars by now. I want you with Esther."

His hopes took a happy leap. "Yes, sir," he responded immediately. Reed might be sheriff, and this was his valley, but he would take orders from the highly respected, highly decorated, highly impressive former Admiral Davidson Delta. Especially if those orders involved close proximity with Esther.

Reed pocketed his phone, headed out of his office, and told Allie he was going to the Deltas'. She nodded, a secretive smile on her face, and he all but ran for his truck.

The drive to the valley took far too long. He saw some vehicles congregated at Papa Delta's and he headed in that direction. Jamming the truck in park, he jogged up to the porch and rapped on the door.

Esther's mom, Myrna, opened it wide. She gave him a quick hug. "Thank you for coming, Reed."

"Of course."

She led the way into the great room area where Thor, Maddie, Papa Delta, and Esther were gathered in the kitchen, preparing dinner. Esther glanced his direction and everyone and everything else melted away. Their gazes held, and he thought he could read in those incredible blue eyes that she did need him, that she missed him almost as much as he missed her, and that they had a chance to be together.

Then she looked away, focusing on the onion she was dicing.

"Sheriff," Papa greeted him, striding around and shaking his hand. "Thanks for coming."

"My pleasure, sir." Reed waved at Maddie and Thor.

"Hi, hot sheriff," Maddie purred, winking at him. Maddie was always a tease.

Esther's gaze sharpened on him, then she rolled her eyes and chopped at the onion.

"Hi, brilliant artist," he said back.

Maddie wrinkled her nose. "Um, no. Not quite as fun as my title for you."

"But more accurate." Reed smiled.

"Brilliant, beautiful, slightly flirtatious artist would be more accurate." She pumped her eyebrows, and everyone laughed. Everyone except Esther. Esther was whacking at the onion with her knife as tears formed in her brilliant blue eyes. Was it only the onion she was crying for, or could he flatter himself into thinking she cared for him?

"Thor and I have been talking," Papa said to Reed, pulling the rest of the group's attention from Maddie's teasing and Reed's attention from the brilliant, beautiful Esther. "Garret Thomson might be hidden in the mountains or the Caribbean by now, but he's proven his obsession with killing women who've rejected him."

Reed nodded. There were now nine cases under investigation and four they believed they could absolutely link to Garret Thomson or Robert Bend. The women had not only dated him but had been his dental clients as well.

"So he might come back and try to get at Esther again," Reed surmised. His gut churned at the thought. He wanted Garret to come so he could dismantle him, but he wouldn't risk Esther for anything, even justice. He would protect her no matter what. Would Papa let him stay here with them?

"He's tracking her somehow," Papa mused.

Reed nodded. He'd been stewing on that all day. The guy following them to Sabores on their first date was a red flag he should've delved deeper into, but they'd thought he was only a smitten, heartbroken loser. Then Garret had stolen a car in Lonepeak Valley, so he'd obviously been following them last night. The final clue was Garret finding her outside on the patio furniture last night. How had he known her exact location? It was spooky, especially because she hadn't had her phone on her on their first date or on the patio. It all added up to some kind of tracking device on Esther's person.

Wait a minute. Reed stared at her beautiful face, unease making his gut churn. "Esther, you said he did free dental work on you?"

She blinked at him, tears from the onion making her blue eyes brighter. She nodded.

Reed looked at Papa.

"An RFID implant," Papa said as it clicked in his mind as well.

"In her tooth or her cheek?" Reed asked.

"Probably her cheek. Another dentist might see it in the tooth."

Esther released the knife and the onion and put her hand to her cheek. "You think he implanted a tracking device on me?"

Papa and Reed both nodded.

"What a psycho," Maddie all but yelled. "You have to find this loser!" She hurried to Esther and wrapped an arm around her cousin. Reed wished that could be his job.

"We will, love," Papa reassured her. Then he looked at Reed. "I want to just get it out of her, but he's smart and I'm afraid he's watching her closely enough that he'd know."

Reed worried about that too, but how could they keep Esther safe?

"We need to keep the implant in and take her someplace he *thinks* he can get to her," Papa said.

"Good," Esther said, straightening away from Maddie. "Then I'll thump him again, and this time he won't get away."

"I don't want him near you," Reed gritted out.

"He threatened you too," she said, staring at him with those gorgeous blue eyes he couldn't resist. "You're the one who needs to stay safe."

"That loser can't hurt me."

She jutted out her chin. "Well, he can't hurt me either."

Papa looked back and forth between them. "You're okay having Esther stay at your place?" he asked Reed.

"Sure," Reed said. He'd personally keep Esther safe, they'd catch this guy, and he'd get more time with Esther.

"No way," Esther protested. "I can stay here."

"I don't know if he'd risk coming back here," Papa said. "He has succeeded in killing and getting away with it so he might think he's invincible, but sadly he's also wicked smart or he would have been caught long ago."

Reed pursed his lips. "Would he risk coming back to the valley at all?" His mind scrambled. "What about the Angel Falls Retreat in Lonepeak? We know the owners. I saw individual cabins spread out from the main lodge. Esther and I could check in as if we're on a romantic getaway. If he already wants to kill me, that will really tick him off."

Esther's eyes widened, and his stomach heated up at the concern he saw there. Did she truly care for him?

"Some of you can set up in the surrounding cabins with surveillance on our cabin," he continued. He had to be decisive and pray she'd go for his idea. "We give it a few days and see if he takes the bait."

Papa nodded. "It would feel less risky to him than coming back to our valley. I like it. Call your friends at Angel Falls, have them keep it quiet, no employees knowing what we're doing, and let's see if we can trap this weasel."

"I'm on it." Reed let his gaze stray to Esther.

She stared back. Apprehension and longing warred in her blue eyes.

Alone with Esther in a cabin for a few days? He'd take any time alone with her, even if she claimed their relationship was fake and she didn't need him.

Unfortunately, her family would be listening in to their every conversation and watching them on surveillance. How would that work if he convinced her to kiss him again? Fortunately, her family liked him and he thought they were all rooting for him. He'd have to push the awkwardness of anyone watching aside and focus on getting through to her.

This might be his chance to trap the loser Garret Thomson, and more importantly his chance to win Esther back. He'd keep her physically safe, no matter what.

Now how to convince her to let him love her?

Chapter Twelve

Esther paced the luxurious but far-too-small cabin at Angel Falls Retreat. Just being back in this beautiful valley and especially at this resort had her fixating on the wonderful evening spent with Reed at the restaurant and spa. Unfortunately for her in-danger-of-throwing-herself-at-Reed heart, they were posing as if they were on a romantic retreat. They weren't supposed to leave their cabin, giving Garret every chance to attack them and to think they were having a dreamy tryst, therefore increasing his jealousy and irrationality. They knew he wouldn't give up on killing them, and once he knew they were together, he would have to act.

Her dad, Thor, Greer, and Colt were staying in a cabin as close as they could book on such short notice. Luckily, there were a few cabins available. Gavin and Kari had been incredible and supportive, but Reed and Papa insisted they not move guests around. It was best to keep things as normal as possible so it wouldn't alert Garret that anyone but Esther and Reed were here and to make sure no employees wagged their tongues. Esther could somehow imagine him lurking around the resort.

Garret. The thought of that scum of the earth made her blood boil. Her throat was still tender when she swallowed, her neck had bruising from being strangled, and the whites of her eyes had red dots in them. Did she really have some tracker in her cheek? She unconsciously touched where her cavity was, sickened that he had secretly implanted something when he'd numbed her mouth for the dental work. Then he'd targeted and stalked her, She was even more sickened at the women and men he had killed. More reports came in every few hours of another woman he'd dated and probably killed. He was sickeningly brilliant to have gotten away with so many deaths.

Thankfully, Esther had fought her way free. She wasn't afraid of him. With Reed, her dad, brothers, and cousin watching over them, what could Garret possibly do to her?

Reed came out of the bathroom. He gave her a patient smile as she continued to do circles around the room. Just looking at him made her body warm up and made her wish she hadn't put him in danger. It was interesting that she wasn't afraid for herself, but somehow she thought the tough sheriff was in danger from the nerdy-looking, murderous dentist.

She was also even more concerned about Reed finding out about her OCD. Different people had thrown around the condition OCD in relation to Garret's disturbed behavior, making Esther more embarrassed and anxious. Would the look in Reed's eyes be pity, sadness, disgust, or would he try to "fix" her problem as an alpha male law enforcement personality would be wont to do?

It had been a very long night last night. The cabin was one beautiful open room and a spacious bathroom. The main area had a kitchen nook, a table and chairs, a couch and loveseat, and a huge king-sized bed. The only privacy was in the bathroom. Reed had taken the couch last night—luckily there had been extra sheets, pillows, and blankets in the closet. Esther had guiltily slept in the bed. Reed was doing all of this for her, but no matter how much she protested, he had refused to take the bed.

There had been a funky tension between them as she'd tried to fall asleep. When sleep was elusive, she'd faked it with slow, deep breaths. She'd known he wanted to talk, but what was there to say? Unless she laid all her issues on the table, which would never happen, and he somehow convinced her he could live with her emotional disorder and it would never put him in danger, which she would never believe, they had no future together.

She'd finally crashed in the early morning. Reed had let her sleep in, but then they'd had nothing to do all day except prepare and eat the food they'd brought, play card games, watch movies, pace the cabin, try to exercise with no equipment or space, and philosophize about Garret, what he had done, and what he might do.

She could tell Reed wanted to talk about their relationship and he hoped she hadn't meant it when she'd said it was fake for her. She had lied, but she didn't want to talk about it. It was hard to even imagine trying to explain her past experiences, her issues, and her fears.

If they talked, she'd probably reveal that she loved him, and then he'd never let her walk away. He was a strong, smart, determined man, and he wouldn't want to accept how miserable her condition could make him. Maybe he'd claim he could help her or that they could deal with it together. Whenever she thought of that, she remembered him calming her down as he wiped her feet dry then put on her socks at the waterfall or when he rushed her out of the steam room and helped her take deep breaths until her world had settled.

She pushed all of that away. It might be beautiful how he could help and be there for her, but it wasn't fair to him. She'd never saddle someone with a lifetime of emotional disability. Especially someone like Reed. He deserved a wife who could inspire and lift him and especially support him in his career.

The other odd part of their every interaction in this cabin was that they knew her dad, brothers, or cousin were watching or at least listening in. Before Reed and Esther had arrived and walked in teasing and laughing like the fake lovers they were, her family had mounted cameras and sensors around the cabin. They took turns monitoring the computer in their two-bedroom cabin. She thought she and Reed should've taken the two-bedroom. Then she felt guilty. Her family was here, away from their wives or girlfriends, to protect her and catch a criminal.

The FBI had approved of the plan. Big surprise. Esther wanted to know what ex-Admiral Davidson Delta would have to propose for the government not to do his bidding.

She and Reed had already eaten and cleaned up dinner and so she was pacing, trying to burn off some energy, and biding her time until she could go to sleep. Maybe she could pretend she fell asleep on the couch so he would have to sleep in the bed.

Reed stood and strode around with her. "Is it helping?"

"Not really, but I cannot handle sitting around much more." Not being able to leave was making her feel out of control. Reed being so irresistible should make her feel the same, but somehow he strengthened and calmed her despite how he made her emotions and desire for him soar.

He smiled. "Maybe tomorrow we could talk our protectors into letting us go on a hike. I know they all took turns today going to the hotel gym and going on mountain bike rides and hikes."

Esther's phone buzzed. She pulled it out. "Thor," she told Reed drily.

"Oh, I can only guess what he's saying."

"Yep." She shook her head and read aloud, "'We've also taken turns getting massages and using the hydrotherapy. That spa is incredible. I'm bringing Shelly back here soon. Plus the restaurant is crazy delicious. Oh, sorry. I forgot you two are cooking your own food.'"

"Wow." Reed looked to where a camera was mounted. "Thanks for rubbing it in."

They'd decided to only order room service occasionally, so if Garret did decide to make his move, he wouldn't be foiled by a worker coming around. Maybe if they could talk her family into a hike, they could also talk them into her and Reed going to the restaurant for dinner. If Garret was around and watching closely at all, wouldn't he think it was a little strange they never left the room?

Esther glanced over at Reed's handsome profile and well-built frame and her face flushed. If they were married, she wouldn't want to leave the room.

But would Garret believe Esther would be holed up in a cabin doing ... stuff with a man she wasn't married to? He'd tried to push boundaries the one time they'd kissed at the end of their third date. She'd shut him down and walked away. Her family thought it would make him even angrier if he thought she was being intimate with Reed.

She blushed again. She couldn't think *intimate* and *Reed* in the same sentence. Especially stuck alone with him and with night coming on.

The thought of her dad, a brother, or cousin seeing them kiss helped cool her down.

"You okay?" Reed asked as they kept walking.

"Oh, sure." Thank heavens he couldn't read her thoughts.

Her phone buzzed again. She pulled it out, wondering what Thor would tease her with this time.

Just so you know, sis, I'm on surveillance duty until ten and then Colt is watching the cameras until two in the morning, so if you need to kiss our boy, neither one of us will watch or report back to Dad or Papa about it. Just give us a thumbs-up and we'll turn away.

Oh, boy.

Very funny, she typed back, then shoved her phone into her pocket.

"What's he saying now?" Reed asked.

She glanced at him and thankfully he wasn't giving her a look that said he'd read the text. She shook her head and looked at the camera. "That he is one pathetic loser ... no offense."

Reed laughed at her quoting a silly teenage movie.

Her phone beeped.

"How much do you want to bet he said, 'None taken'?" she asked.

Reed smiled and lowered his voice so the cameras couldn't pick it up. "I'll bet you a kiss."

Her face heated again. "What?"

"If he says 'none taken' like you think he will, quoting that movie, then I'll ... rub your feet for you."

Esther really liked her feet rubbed, but the thought of Reed rubbing them sounded almost as intimate as a kiss and reminded her of him sweetly wiping her feet dry and putting her socks on that day at the waterfall.

His dark eyes stared into hers, and their pacing slowed and then stopped.

"If he has any other reply, you have to give me a kiss," he repeated quietly.

Esther's heart beat high and fast. "So basically there are a million responses out there he could give and where you will win this bet."

Reed gave her a slow grin. "Yes, ma'am. But you and I both know he probably texted exactly what you think he did. I've heard him say that line a hundred times to Aiden."

Esther tried to slow her breathing. Reed was right. Thor's twin Aiden was in the SEALs and they rarely saw him. Thor held out hope Aiden would make his wedding but Aiden had made no promises. Both of her brothers had loved that stupid movie and quoted it all the time.

The bet was fine and a fun way to keep their minds distracted. Reed was simply teasing with her, and Thor was helping them get through this weird time by sending funny texts. She knew her brother well, and she knew Reed was probably right. Thor would've texted back, *none taken*. She absolutely knew he would. A foot rub sounded like heaven right now, and she'd just keep it from getting too ... personal. It would be fine.

"Okay," she heard herself say.

Reed's grin got even bigger, crinkling his eyes and the skin around his mouth.

She pulled out her phone, chagrined that her fingers were trembling. This was the exact opposite of her usual control, but instead of being concerned, she felt alive and invigorated. Even the thought of kissing Reed again had her pulse racing. Their kiss on the sidewalk not that many days ago had been to get Garret off her back and shouldn't have been incredible with his deputies, Garret, and who knew how many other people watching, but it had been. It had been impossibly incredible. In the spa the other night, their lips had barely gotten tangled before Gavin had interrupted. She wanted to kiss him again, wanted it so badly that she found herself hoping Thor hadn't given the standard response. It wasn't smart and it would lead to heartache for both of them, but she ached to feel his mouth take possession of hers again.

She swiped up and clicked on the text app. Thor's text stream was still open, and his answer made her jaw drop wide.

Plenty of offense taken. You'll be the pathetic loser if you don't kiss Reed.

She blinked and looked at Reed. Luckily, he wasn't craning his neck to read their texts or he'd see Thor's other text telling her that he wouldn't watch while she kissed Reed as well as this one. She would accuse him and Reed of setting this up, but she didn't believe Reed had seen either text.

"What did he say?" Reed had a look of anticipation and hope on his face. She loved that he wasn't looking at the text. She could lie to him ... but she wouldn't.

She drew in a breath and admitted, "He said 'plenty of offense taken'."

Reed's eyes widened and then he let out a whoop. It was adorable how excited he was. If it was possible for a tough, handsome, smart sheriff to look adorable.

"Now, sweetie." She backed up, mind racing to think of a way to save herself. "Let's just calm down here for a minute."

Her phone was beeping texts, but she wasn't about to look at them. Reed matched her step for step, coming toward her like the alpha male he was, tough and irresistible and ready to claim his prize.

"Now, sweetie," he repeated in a husky drawl. "A bet's a bet. I've never known a Delta to go back on their word."

Her heart was racing so fast she put a hand on her chest. She backed into the side wall and stopped. Reed stopped too, giving her a few feet as if he didn't want to make her feel trapped, but the way he was looking at her ... whew. He could start a forest fire with that look.

"Reed, honey, I do keep my word, but ..." What could she say? She'd made the stupid bet, and she wanted his kiss. She just didn't know how to deal with the aftermath. She bit at her lip.

He let out a low groan. "Love ... if you keep doing that, I'm going to kiss you without your permission."

Esther's eyes widened, both at how taken he seemed to be with her and the fact that he would still wait for her permission before he kissed her. "You're not going to just claim your prize? You'll still wait for my permission?"

He was so confident and strong, but Reed could obviously sense how stirred up she was inside, that she'd gone through something horrific in the past, and he would never take advantage of her in any way.

He smiled softly. "I might tease you about not fulfilling our bet" —his smile slid away—"but I want you to *want* to kiss me, Esther. I want you to want it as badly as I do."

Her stomach did a flip-flop and her entire body felt full of fire and longing. She was terrified to say the words that could eventually break her in two, but she wanted to kiss Reed. The desire for him seemed to consume her, and she told herself she could deal with the emotional rollercoaster ... later.

Before she could second-guess herself for the hundredth time, she admitted, "I want to kiss you so badly it's all I can think about."

Reed's dark eyes reflected the same longing she felt inside. Then a slow smile tilted his appealing lips.

She quivered, anticipation thrumming through her body. This was going to be the kiss to end all kisses. She knew it, and she couldn't stand the wait for one more second. She leaned toward him.

Reed turned, and he walked away from her.

What was happening? Esther leaned against the wall for support. Disappointment and the need to be in Reed's arms made her weak. Was he going to kiss her, or not? She couldn't handle all the emotions ripping through her for much longer.

The crazy thing was ... she tried to keep emotional rollercoasters out of her life so she wouldn't revert to OCD tendencies or embarrass herself or others ... but with Reed and their banter and the anticipation for his kiss, she found she loved the emotions surging through her. She didn't think they would hurt or mess her or Reed up. Then again, they might. She'd have to shelve that and deal with it later.

Right now, she wanted Reed to claim his kiss.

Reed shut off the overhead lights on the panel by the door. The room was lit only by a lamp next to the couch. The cameras would have a harder time picking up their movements, and it was even more romantic.

Turning back toward her, Reed gave her a significant look that should've made her collapse on the floor, but instead it strengthened her. He wanted her, and her kiss, and she was everything to him.

Walking slowly toward her, Reed pulled out his phone, held down the side button, and said, "Text Thor."

"What would like you me to say to Thor, the true hero of Summit Valley?" his phone said back.

Esther smiled, though her legs were trembling. She was certain Thor had programmed that into Reed's phone. Her number for Thor was simply Most Heroic Brother Ever. Her other brothers, besides Greer, gave Thor a hard time about it.

"Don't look at the cameras," Reed said into his phone, giving her a brilliant smirk, "Unless you want to watch me kiss your sister thoroughly."

Esther arched her eyebrows, trying to look brave. "Thoroughly?" she asked, voice cracking.

Reed pocketed his phone, ignoring the beep of a text back from Thor. He approached her like the strong, confident, incredible man he was. He rested one hand on the wall by her head and leaned in until his chest brushed hers.

"Thoroughly," he repeated in a low, sexy growl as his gaze focused on her lips.

Esther smiled, and she found the strength to say sassily, "Well, get to fulfilling this bet ... thoroughly."

He tenderly cupped her cheek with his free hand, his thumb trailing across her lower lip and making her feel faint and out of breath.

"I just need you to know," he said softly. "This kiss has nothing to do with fake dating, a bet, or anything but the fact that I am head over heels in love with you, Esther Delta."

Esther's eyes widened at his beautiful proclamation. He loved her?

He loved her.

The smart thing to do would be to duck away from his touch or tell him to stop. She knew he would honor her request. She should do any of a hundred things to stop this out-of-control love bus from crashing off a cliff. The last thing she should do was kiss him, let him kiss her, and in that husky voice as he'd said, kiss her "thoroughly."

Instead of being one bit smart, she ignored all the warnings screaming in her head, arched up, and met him halfway as he bent and captured her lips with his.

The kiss was long and thorough and had her lips singing with pleasure and her mind vacant of anything but one hot sheriff—*her* sheriff—Reed. She loved him, and if she could push away all the fears of the future and of Garret somehow hurting him, she might tell him that.

After she kept kissing him and kissing him and kissing him.

Reed pinned her against the wall and fulfilled that wish, kissing her with a passion she'd never experienced in her life. He wrapped his hands around her waist and lifted her off the ground. She clung to him, and they kept kissing. Never had she kissed someone this deeply and thoroughly. This should feel completely out of control, but she loved every second. She'd never been so happy, carefree, and worried less about control in her life.

Reed easily carried her to the couch and all thoughts of anything but him disappeared. He settled down and cradled her against his chest as the kisses continued. The love she felt for him and from him grew into a frenzied crescendo. She'd never have to deal with her issues or worries again. She'd keep clinging to Reed, kissing him, and nothing in this world could touch her.

Her phone started ringing and buzzing in her pocket. She ignored it. Then Reed's phone started ringing and she could feel it buzzing against her hip. She prayed he'd ignore it. Her phone started ringing again.

Reed slowed the kisses and gently pulled away with a beautiful smile on his lips. "Not that I would interrupt kissing you for anything, but with the situation we're in, we should answer one of our phones."

"I hate rational thoughts," she said, and she meant it. She didn't want rational thoughts, danger, or the world to intrude on their incredible kissing connection. Most especially, she didn't want her usual worries or barriers to return.

He smiled and pulled out his phone, leaning slightly back on the couch and looking so irresistible she wanted to kiss him all over again. She slid off his lap so she wouldn't attack him while he made the phone call. He frowned slightly at her movement and tucked her into his side with his strong arm. She didn't mind. She leaned into his shoulder and listened.

"Hey, Thor. Oh?" Reed's voice suddenly sounded a little chagrined. "Okay. That's ... reasonable. Tell him I apologize and of course I'll treat her with respect tonight."

Esther grimaced and looked up at him. "My dad?" she mouthed.

He nodded. "Talk to you tomorrow." He hung up and slid his phone back in his pocket, pulling a face at her. "Apparently Thor was on camera duty and respectfully trying *not* to watch us 'mack-daddy,' but ... your dad walked by the screen. He said to cool it or he'd come over here and kick my butt."

"Yikes." She looked him over. "I think he could do it, too."

Reed chuckled, then reached over and flipped off the lamp. The room plunged into darkness. "If he can't see us ..." He let the words dangle there.

Esther's heart took off again. She was surprised Reed would disregard her dad's instructions like that. He pulled her tighter to his side, but instead of devouring her mouth again like she longed for him to do, he tucked her head against his shoulder and tenderly trailed his fingers across her back.

"I'm just kidding. That was ..." His voice got deeper. "Incredible. I'll wait until we're married to kiss you that passionately again."

Esther wanted nothing more than to cuddle close to him all night. Well, unless she could kiss him passionately again. But "wait until we're married"? She'd pushed all her fears aside earlier and let herself kiss him long and far too deeply, and now look what had happened. She'd had her moment of fun and now it would mess them both up.

She tugged away from him and murmured, "Bathroom," then stumbled across the dark room.

Reed flipped the lamp back on and stood. Esther whirled around to face him, and he splayed his hands. "Esther ... I don't want to scare you away."

Too late. She'd gotten completely out of control kissing him so desperately. Was that all bad? If it hurt him when she flipped out, it would be. Was she flipping out? Not yet.

She forced a smile before he saw how her mind was stewing. "You didn't. I just need to ... use the restroom and then ... get some sleep."

"Sweetheart ..."

Esther hurried into the bathroom and shut the door. Luckily, the closet was attached to the bathroom, so she could get dressed after she took a long, long bath. Maybe she could use some of the extra pillows and blankets in the closet and make a bed in there. She turned on the huge tub.

"Esther, please," Reed said through the door.

She pretended not to hear him, watching the tub fill with water. Drops of water landed on the surface below her face and she realized tears had worn trails down her face and off her chin. She put a finger to her lips and let herself relive those kisses. If only she wasn't such an emotional mess. Yet with Reed she didn't feel like a mess—not until she let the real world or her own brain intrude.

"Love," he called softly to her.

Esther squeezed her eyes shut. How was she going to face him again? How would she keep herself from kissing him and somehow convince him they weren't meant to be together?

Why *couldn't* they be together? All the reasons were blurry, and she was too consumed with Reed to think clearly. Which wasn't smart as Garret could come after them and hurt Reed.

Ah, Reed. Had any man ever been so incredible? It was going to seriously mess her up to break away from him—again—but better now before she got any deeper.

Had she really thought she loved Roman? His kisses and the feelings she'd had for him were nothing compared to this. And though she felt guilt for his death and for being obsessive with him, she recognized it had been a college romance that would've burned out if he hadn't died.

Could she explain to Reed what she'd been through and what she still dealt with far too often? She knew he'd tell her he'd be there for her no matter what. She loved that she knew that, but she wanted to be strong on her own.

Yet what had she spent the last ten years doing? She'd proved she was strong on her own. She was accomplished and successful.

Was it finally time to trust herself and to trust Reed? Would love mess her up, or could it strengthen her even further? Could it make her a better Delta Protection Detail member? A better lawyer? A better person? Someday, a better wife and mother? She would definitely be a happier person if she could be by Reed's side.

What was fair to Reed? He seemed to be completely gone over her. Could she trust his instincts and feelings as well as her own?

She bowed her head and prayed. Maybe she had no answers of her own, but it was clear that she loved and wanted to be with Reed. She needed heavenly instruction to know the best way to proceed.

Chapter Thirteen

Reed wanted to bang his fists against the bathroom door. He heard the water running in the tub and knew Esther was shutting him out.

Walking away from the bathroom, he paced the main room again. Their kisses and connection were off the charts, but still she kept pushing him away. What was it? What had happened to her? How could he help her heal?

And find whoever had wounded her and take the guy apart.

His phone rang, and he ripped it out. Thor. "Hey," he muttered.

"Wow." Thor chuckled. "That was some kissing. Shelly and I's kisses are off the charts too. I wonder if they look like that."

"I thought you weren't going to watch."

"Well, when my dad walked back in and started going insane, I thought I'd better watch so I could testify to the judge if he came over and shot you through the heart."

Reed laughed shortly and pushed a hand at his hair. "Thanks for helping me avoid that."

"Sure. You're my friend. So, you and my big sis, huh? Is she the coolest ever?"

"She is," Reed agreed. "But Thor ..." Should he share with her brother? He wanted Esther's trust more than anything, but he feared he'd never have it.

"Yeah?" Thor said into the pause.

Reed shook his head. He couldn't say anything. "Sorry, I can't."

"She's trying to ditch you?" Thor guessed.

Reed could only grunt. Why couldn't he ever be enough for Esther? Why couldn't she confide in him and love him like he loved her?

"Sorry, man," Thor said. "I wish I had some good advice or something."

Reed wished he did too.

"You know I support you." Thor huffed out a heavy breath. "I adore my sis so much. If she'd just ..." He broke off, and Reed was glad he did. He wanted to know what was keeping him and Esther apart, but he wanted her to be the one to trust him with it. "Are you going to give up on her?"

"Never," Reed said so vehemently it surprised even him.

"Thank you." Thor released a breath. "I was afraid you'd get sick of it. You know how hard I pursued Shelly."

"I do." Reed had been friends with both of them for a lot of years.

"It was ... rough, but now? So worth it, man. So worth it."

Reed felt that course through him. He was good at being patient. Esther was worth any amount of patience he had to exercise. He opened his mouth to thank his friend—

Bullets slammed into the exterior of the cabin. Glass shattered.

Reed dropped the phone and dove for his pistol on the kitchen table. The two windows on the north side of the cabin had numerous holes in them, and the one was half gone. The bathroom had a window on that same side. Had Garret shot it out as well?

Reed grabbed his pistol and raced for the bathroom door.

"No!" Esther screamed, the sound muffled.

Reed yanked on the handle. Locked. He kicked the door, but it didn't budge. Growling in frustration, he backed up and shot at the lock, then kicked it in. The door finally flew open to reveal Garret trying to shove Esther out the broken window. She was fighting back beautifully. She was still in her T-shirt and shorts.

"Let her go!" Reed hollered, rushing toward them.

"Stop!" Garret squealed, shoving his pistol into Esther's neck.

Reed stopped mid-stride and raised his hands, his pistol in his right hand. He was only two feet away. Did he dare leap at them, or would Garret fire? They knew this guy had killed repeatedly. Reed couldn't risk Esther.

"Back up," Garret instructed. "Drop your gun."

Reed could hear footsteps pounding their way. Thor, Greer, Keith, and Colton would be here soon. He backed up and set the gun on the nearby counter. He wouldn't risk it going off and hurting Esther if he dropped it.

Esther's blue eyes were fully focused on Reed. Could he somehow signal her? He had to protect her at all costs. "My family will be here any second," Esther said evenly. "You'd better run like the wimp you are."

Reed had to admire her bravery, though it terrified him to have her in danger like this. This guy had shown no qualms about murdering the women he'd dated.

"After I kill you both," Garret sneered.

"Shoot me first." Reed prayed Esther would get away if given the chance. Then he could shoot Garret.

"Gladly." Garret whipped the gun from Esther's neck.

It was the only opening Reed needed. He swept his gun off the counter.

Garret fired.

Fire ripped through Reed's abdomen. He was flung back against the counter, and the back of his head exploded with pain. The world turned red first, then black.

Chapter Fourteen

"No!" Esther screamed, watching her worst nightmare come true as blood blossomed along the bottom of Reed's T-shirt as he went down.

The memory of blood covering Roman's chest pierced her, but she shoved it away and focused. She elbowed Garret hard, grabbed his arm, and flipped him over face-first onto the tile floor. Garret's forehead smacked the tile and his body went limp. She went down on one knee and slammed her elbow into the back of his neck just to be certain he was out.

Thor and her dad rushed into the bathroom first. Colt and Greer must be outside securing the area.

Esther scrambled to Reed's side, checking his pulse first. She felt the reassuring thrum. "He has a pulse."

Her dad went to Garret's side and pointed his gun at him even though he wasn't moving. He pulled out his phone with the other hand and instructed, "Call 911."

Thor grabbed a clean white hand towel from the stack in the bathroom and dropped to Reed's other side, lifting his shirt and examining the wound before pressing the towel against his side. "Bullet wound to the side of the abdomen. It looks clean."

Esther leaned down. Reed's warm breath touched her cheek. "He's breathing."

She heard her dad repeating everything to the dispatcher. "Has a pulse, breathing on his own, gunshot wound to the side of the abdomen that looks clean, putting pressure on it, unconscious ..."

"Is he unconscious because of the shot or blood loss?" Esther asked Thor. She was steady, composed, and her only focus was on Reed being all right. Dimly, she realized it was the opposite of her experience with Roman, but she didn't have time to dwell on it.

He shook his head. "I don't think so. Did he hit his head?"

"Yes. He hit his head on the counter," she remembered with a breath of relief. He was still in danger, but hitting his head was much better than losing consciousness from a bullet wound that quickly. She gently probed at the back of his head and felt a large knot. "Head wound most likely the cause of lack of consciousness rather than the gunshot wound," she reported to her dad.

Garret stirred and opened his eyes. Her dad bent low and grasped the man's shirt, shoving him into the tile and then digging his knee into the man's chest. "You tried to hurt my daughter. I will kill you if you so much as blink."

Esther had never heard her dad threaten someone like that. She knew he was trained to kill and could easily take out Garret, but it warmed her heart to hear him be so protective.

Garret's eyes went wide. He didn't move.

"Esther ..."

Esther's gaze darted back to Reed.

His dark eyes fluttered open, and he murmured, "I love you." Then his eyes rolled back in his head.

Esther's heart gave a strange turn and her body filled with happiness. He loved her. She already knew—he'd told her before he kissed her that it was because he'd fallen in love with her—but he'd been willing to sacrifice himself for her in the showdown with Garret.

He was unconscious, and they'd been through something traumatic. She should be completely falling apart in this out-of-control situation. Reed had almost died. Her heart raced at the thought, but she didn't go into panic mode or start muttering or run screaming from the building or pound on his chest and demand that he live.

She looked at his hand lying on the hard tile floor and lifted it into her lap. The feel of his palm warm against hers brought peace. The depth of her love for him calmed and lifted her. Him telling her he loved her only strengthened it. On her own, she had proven herself to be strong. She would be even stronger with Reed, holding his hand, teasing with him, discussing law, laughing and teasing together. Now he just had to be all right and wake up so she could tell him how much she loved him. She sent a silent prayer that he would be okay.

Thor pumped his eyebrows at her. "My buddy loves you. Don't ditch him, sis. Please."

Esther ignored her brother, but the last thing she was planning right now was how to ditch Reed. She clung to his hand as desperately as she clung to the prayers running through her head.

Colt and Greer crowded into the already crowded bathroom. "The perimeter is secure," Colt reported. "He was alone."

Her dad nodded. "The police and an ambulance are coming. Could you talk to the dispatcher?" He tilted his head toward the phone, not moving from pinning Garret down.

Colt grabbed the phone and started talking as Gavin Strong appeared over Greer's shoulder.

Esther focused on Reed's handsome face, trailing her fingertips along the back of his hand, praying he would wake up again and praying the wound to his head or his abdomen wasn't serious.

Thankfully he was breathing, had a strong pulse, and it looked like Thor had the bleeding under control.

She couldn't believe how in control she felt. She'd faced her worst fears, seeing the man she loved shot because of her, unconscious and bloody, and she'd helped take care of him and focused on her faith and love to get her through.

The ambulance and police arrived quickly. Esther stood back as they loaded Reed up and started an IV. She saw his eyes flutter open, and he glanced around. "Esther," he called out.

"I'm here, sweetheart." She hurried back to his side and wrapped her hand around his.

He looked at her hand and then back at her face. He smiled. "I love you."

"Oh, Reed." Her heart threatened to burst with love for him. Before she could tell him she loved him too, his eyes closed again and his breathing evened out.

The paramedics were busy shuttling Reed to the ambulance. She followed, and one of them smiled at her. "You can ride with us."

"Thank you." She waited while they loaded the ambulance and then climbed in.

Reed didn't wake again on the long ride to Aspen. Apparently Lonepeak's medical center was small and Reed was stable enough to handle the forty-five-minute ride to the larger city. The "stable" prognosis was a very good one.

They reached the hospital and Esther watched them unload Reed and start to wheel him away.

"Esther," she heard him croak out.

She rushed to keep up with the stretcher. "I'm here, sweetie," she told him, trying to reach for him, but they were moving fast.

"I love you," he said.

The paramedics laughed.

"I think he needs to hear it back," the one who'd told her she could ride with them said.

Esther looked down at Reed's handsome face as she jogged to keep up and he was rolled into the emergency room. His eyes were closed again. She wanted to tell him she loved him, but not until he was lucid and they were alone.

They rolled him into an exam room and a nurse kindly escorted her to the waiting area. She paced and chewed on her nails and prayed and paced some more. Thor, Colt, Greer, and her dad were all there watching her and offering her drinks, snacks, and hugs. Well, Greer never offered more than a side squeeze, but he smiled kindly at her.

Papa, Reed's mom and stepdad, her mom, Maddie, her uncle and aunt, Bailey, Shelly, Klein, Alivia, Jessie, and then Reed's two younger brothers all arrived. Everyone was hugging, asking for the story, listening to Thor embellish and make everyone laugh. Esther tried to participate and laugh, but she was ready to see Reed awake and healthy and finally, finally tell him she loved him. Then she had to share her past and figure out their future together.

A man in surgeon scrubs came through the emergency room doors. He looked around at the crowd. "Who is the closest of kin to Sheriff Reed Peterson?" he asked.

Reed's mom, Heather, stepped forward, her husband close to her side. Esther couldn't even remember Reed's stepdad's name. She hadn't been around when they'd gotten married, and her brain was overwrought right now. She wanted to claim she was the love of Reed's life and step forward with his mom, but sadly she didn't have medical power of attorney or any kind of legal document backing up her claim.

"I am," Heather said. "But everyone here is kin. You can tell us all what you need to say."

Esther appreciated that. She was amazed and grateful at how

steady she felt despite the angst of wanting to be with Reed and know he was all right and see for herself that he would fully recover. Even with Reed not by her side, he strengthened her with his love and devotion to her. He had never given up on her, even when she'd pushed him away. Ah, she loved him. Now to tell him that and kiss him without her dad watching on the cameras.

The doctor nodded. "He's stable."

A collective breath whooshed out. Esther leaned to the side and found Papa right there, slipping his arm around her and holding her up with an understanding smile.

"The surgery went well. The bullet passed through the oblique muscle but didn't damage any internal organs. We believe the contusion on the back of his head is to blame for him passing out and his repetitive dialogue, not the blood loss. He should wake from sedation soon and then we'll know if he has a concussion."

Several people murmured, "Thank you," and "Thanks, Doc."

He nodded his welcome. "Why don't you come with me, Mom and Dad, and the nurse will take you to the recovery room. They'll have him in there soon."

Heather gave everyone a nod and said, "Thanks for being here."

Esther forced a smile at her. There was no other place she'd rather be.

His mom and stepdad followed the doctor. The rest of the group started talking again and then slowly one or two said the rounds of goodbyes and headed out. Colt reassured her he and Bailey would pack up her and Reed's stuff from the cabin and get it back home for them. She gave each person a hug.

Within the hour, it was down to Esther, her parents, Papa, Thor and Shelly, and Reed's brothers.

Heather appeared at the emergency room entrance. Everyone stood and surged toward her. She gave a quick smile around the group, but focused on Esther. "He's woken up several times."

"Praise the good Lord," Esther's mom said.

"Every time he says, 'Esther, I love you,' then he falls back asleep." Heather's dark eyes, so similar to her son's, were sparkling with happiness. She started forward and gathered Esther in a hug. Esther returned the embrace. "The doctor's worried that it's a sign of concussion, but I looked into his eyes. They're clear. He just wants there to be no doubt that he loves you, so he says it every time he wakes up. Do you love him back, sweet girl?"

Esther bit at her lip. She could not say it in front of everybody. She had to tell him first. "Can I go sit with him?"

"Of course." Heather's gaze registered disappointment that she wouldn't claim she loved him, but she tugged her forward.

"We'll be here waiting," her dad said to their backs. "No making out like last night."

There were several chuckles at that. Esther's neck heated. She turned around and flung at her dad, "You won't be able to watch this time."

His eyes widened in surprise, and then her mom and Thor laughed louder than ever.

She strode into the emergency room with Heather, hoping his mom wouldn't reference her dad's comment.

"Making out with my boy, eh?" she asked.

They skirted down a side hallway. "He's a great kisser," Esther admitted.

They reached an open door with a curtain inside shielding the occupants. "Is that all he is to you? A good kisser?"

Esther met her gaze. "He's so much more, but I need to tell him everything and it's very, very complicated." Strangely enough, it didn't feel complicated. Not anymore. Though she'd been terrified when Reed was shot, she'd reacted in a calm, decisive manner. She was okay, and Reed was incredible.

Heather's gaze softened on her. "It always is, love."

"Esther," she heard Reed's deep, wonderful voice call from inside the room. "I love you."

Heather smiled. "It's not just the head injury talking." She pushed her toward the curtain. "Be good to my boy."

Esther walked around the curtain and saw Reed's strong form stretched out on a too-small hospital bed. His stepdad smiled up at her, then stood. He squeezed her hand and said, "He's repeated that over a dozen times."

"Do you think it's the head injury?" Esther asked quietly, looking at Reed, but he appeared to be back asleep.

Reed's stepdad shrugged his shoulders. "The head injury might be why he's repeating it, but it's not at the root of why he's saying it."

Esther's heart beat quicker. It was time to tell him everything.

Reed's mom and stepdad both smiled at her. Heather hugged her again quick and then they both disappeared around the curtain.

Esther rushed to Reed's side. His color looked good. He somehow looked more handsome than ever. The sheet was only up to his waist, revealing his beautiful chest and a large bandage covering the side of his abdomen. An IV was the only tube attached to his arm. That was good.

She sank into the chair pulled up by his bedside. She put her hand on his cheek and savored the feel of his warm cheek under a day's growth. "Reed," she said softly.

He stirred and said without opening his eyes, "Esther?"

"Yes, sweetie, I'm here." She wrapped her fingers around his. If he was really awake, he'd know what that meant to her.

His hand tightened around hers. "Esther ..." His eyes opened and his dark gaze penetrated through her. He was definitely awake. "I love you." He said the words slowly and deliberately. There was no doubt how sincere he was.

Esther's heart fluttered. Those words would never get old coming from Reed. "I know," she said.

He chuckled, then his gaze got far too serious. "I was hoping for ... something more."

She smiled. "There's so much more I need to tell you, so much I want to share. Are you awake enough or should I wait?"

"I've been in and out of it, fighting to wake up. I've been waiting and hoping you'd come." He brushed his thumb along the back of her hand. "Hoping for this. Are you ready to ... tell me?"

"Yes." It should've been scary, but all she wanted was to be close to Reed and share everything. He wouldn't judge her, he'd never stop loving her, and he was so devoted to her there wasn't even a worry about how to phrase it or what to say or not say. "I was so scared when you got shot. I thought I'd flip out, but I didn't."

"Of course you didn't. You're so brave and impressive, Esther."

"I haven't always been," she admitted. "But I realized that I have learned over the past ten years how to be in control and in charge of my emotions, and there's also the fact that I'm so deeply in love with you. *You* strengthen and calm me." She clung to his hand and brushed her other hand along his jaw and into his hair. He smiled at her.

"You're incredible Reed," she continued. "You're everything to me and everything I've ever wanted. You're steady, tough, kind, smart, fun—"

"Not to mention a hot sheriff," Reed said.

"And so humble," she teased. "For a guy with a head injury who's been in and out of lucidity, you are *very* with it."

He looked down at their joined hands and said seriously, "I not only had a great reason to get my mind clear quick, but I had someone to guide me here and let me know things would be okay."

She marveled at those words. That was exactly what he'd done for her—guided her and loved her and assured her it would be okay if he was with her.

Reed raised their clasped hands, softly brushing her knuckles with his lips. "Do you really love me, Esther?"

She stared at him and admitted, "I do. I love you and I love everything about you."

"I think I've repeated about a hundred times how much I love you. I had to make sure you knew." His cheeks crinkled into a grin. "But I'll say it again. I love you, Esther."

She grinned as happiness blossomed inside her. She had to tell him ... everything. "Can I tell you a long story?"

He lowered their joined hands to the bed. "I would love to hear any story. Please forgive me if I fall asleep on you, though."

She grunted out a laugh. "I don't think that's a good line for our hero."

He smiled. "As long as I am your hero. If I recall, all I did was get shot. Who beat up Garret?"

"Me." She pumped her eyebrows.

"That's my girl."

Esther wanted to be his girl. She wanted it more than anything. But she had to tell him everything first. "Okay, short version. I fell in love at nineteen. He told me I was too obsessed and I couldn't leave him alone. It turns out he was right, and I lost control. He was a policeman, and I called and texted him dozens of times the night he broke it off. I was immature and thought if I could just see him, we could work it out."

Reed nodded encouragingly.

Nerves fluttered in her stomach, but she reminded herself he wouldn't judge her. "I tracked his phone and went to see him, took him his favorite brownies."

It hurt to remember it all so vividly. It was also humiliating to have Reed hear all of this. She kept reminding herself she had matured and gotten so much stronger. Awful things happened sometimes. She wished she could change it, but she couldn't.

Reed waited.

"When he saw me, he tried to get me out of the situation. They were shadowing a heroin exchange, waiting to make a bust, and I was about to mess up the entire thing. It was in a nice neighborhood, so I had no idea I was in danger." She took a quick breath. "One of the men saw Roman coming for me, realized the police were watching them, and shot Roman in the back."

Reed's eyes widened, and he didn't look like he was going to fall asleep, not at all. "Esther," he murmured. But even in that moment he looked concerned about her, not disgusted or frustrated with her lack of self-control or interference in a drug bust that caused a policeman to die.

"Everything went crazy. Roman's partner called in the shooting and tried to follow the perpetrator." She licked her lips. "I had first aid training, but I was in shock and I froze. I didn't put pressure on the wound or assess Roman or anything I could've done to possibly save his life."

Reed clung to her hand, his eyes steady on hers. She saw no judgment there, and it encouraged her to keep going.

"Roman died before the EMTs arrived. Then I honestly went crazy. Papa and my parents are the only ones who know what happened. I spent my sophomore year of college in therapy and I spent longer than that trying to forgive myself for causing Roman's death."

"Esther," Reed said softly. His dark gaze was as serious as it had ever been. "The dealer killed Roman, not you."

A tear raced past her lashes, and she wiped it away with her free hand. "I shouldn't have even been there. I made Roman leave his safe spot and then I did nothing to save his life."

He nodded. "It's awful what happened, but we've all made mistakes. And your innocent mistake and then freezing in a horrific situation does not make a tragic death your fault. It just makes it a tragedy, and even harder to deal with." The look in his eyes said he knew she'd struggled and maybe still did.

"Thank you, Reed." She sniffled, then rushed on. "I was diagnosed with OCD and panic attacks. I learned how to prevent the panic attacks and manage or use the OCD for good habits and rules that helped me, but I was terrified that if I fell in love again, the minute things got rocky I would get out of control and act insane again. That I would not only hurt the person I loved and myself, but also be a detriment to my family and the Delta secret. The fact that you're the sheriff and in the line of danger made me even more afraid to admit my love for you."

Reed pushed the button to incline the bed a bit and shifted up in it. His chest and arm muscles flexed. "Esther, I am so sorry. I shouldn't have pushed you. I had no idea what you'd been through and what you've had to overcome. How can I be there for you?"

She smiled. "You are there for me, Reed. I don't know if you remember in your current condition, but at the waterfall when I freaked out, you didn't judge me. You gently dried my feet, put my socks on, and promised not to ask questions. In the steam room, when I went nuts, you calmly got me out of there and acted like it was no big deal."

"It wasn't. You're amazing, Esther, and I want to be there for you any way I can."

"I know you do. It was ... surprising tonight. When you were shot and my worst fear came true—the man I love being shot because of me—I reacted calmly and did what I've been trained to do in an emergency, taking your pulse, checking your breath, checking your head injury while Thor staunched the bleeding and my dad called 911."

"Good girl. I'm so proud of you."

"Thank you, but I believe it's you. Even when you were knocked out and bleeding from a bullet wound, my love for you kept me calm and focused. Once I'd done all I could do, I took your hand, and it made all the difference."

He squeezed her hand.

"With you by my side, I can stay in control and keep using my OCD tendencies to work hard and be successful, but not get obsessed or hurt myself or others because of it." She smiled tenderly at him. "Though I am kind of obsessed with my hot sheriff."

"I'm glad to hear it." He tugged her toward him. "I'm obsessed, committed to, and deeply in love with my beautiful, smart, fun, incredible lawyer."

Their lips met. Esther let go of her need for control and kissed him the way she longed to. Her dad wasn't watching, and nothing had ever felt so good as Reed's lips taking possession of hers, especially knowing they loved each other and she was finally putting her worries and fears to rest and focusing where she should ... on her hot sheriff.

Mrs. Esther Delta-Peterson.

Their names melded perfectly together in her mind. Reed's kiss was perfect and Reed was perfect, at least for her he was. It turned out Kari had been right. It wasn't about finding the perfect person, or even being perfect herself. It was about finding the right person for her.

Reed's kiss become all-encompassing and she focused on the happiness and joy they could discover ... together.

Excerpt - Compromised

Chapter One

Melene Collier stayed close to her fourteen-year old guide's back as they worked their way along the narrow ocean path. One wrong step and she'd plummet to the surf and the rocks a hundred feet below. Probably a death sentence, but she'd escaped so many death sentences over the years in her humanitarian work, what was one more. *Sorry*, she breathed to the guardian angels her Grandma Larue always claimed she made work overtime, *not trying to make your job harder.*

It was a semi-dark night with a pretty half-moon glinting off the smooth waves of the Baltic Sea. If she wasn't in such a precarious spot she'd savor the beauty. She usually enjoyed the August nights near the coast as she worked in Poland with refugees from the conquered country of Banida, providing them food, shelter, and hope.

Her stomach churned. Hope was getting a little short as Commander Frederick had renamed himself King Frederick and was now setting his sights on Poland. Banida was a small country sandwiched between the northern ends of Germany and Poland. If Frederick had his way, Melene, the other volunteers, and these innocent people in desperate need and already displaced from their homes would be in the middle of a war zone. With no support and no escape.

The path turned inland from the ocean trail and they made their way through thick forest. The path got darker and harder to follow with the tree canopy blocking out the moon's light and them not daring to use a light. An at-risk family was heading their direction from Banida. Melene and Thomas were to assist the mom and her five small children to the relative safety of their camp while the husband went back to try to protect their home and farm and fight with the rebels still attempting to stand up to Frederick.

She shivered even though it wasn't cold. Frederick was evil clear through. The psychopath claimed he was a descendant of Frederick the Great, and the rightful heir of all of Europe. He ruled with intimidation, threats, secret conspiracies, and murder. Melene had heard stories that would give grown men nightmares. In Africa last year, she used to read Michael Vey to the older children and teenagers at nights. They all agreed Dr. Hatch was the most disturbing and evil villain imaginable and she'd often skipped the most disturbing parts of those books.

Sadly the stories about "King" Frederick weren't fiction. It was all too reminiscent of Hitler's rise to power and Melene prayed daily for the blameless people in danger and for the United Nations to pull their heads out of their rears before Frederick grew too strong to stop.

Thomas stopped so quickly Melene ran into his bony back. He steadied her with his arm. They were far enough away from the ocean trail and in thick dense trees. She wasn't in danger of falling off a cliff. Why had he stopped her?

Her ears perked up as she heard voices. The family they were searching for?

Two male voices carried through the trees and she felt instantly disappointed and concerned. These two strong male voices were definitely not their misplaced refugees. One of them had a heavy European accent, possibly German, the other sounded like he was British.

She froze and listened. She realized the voices wouldn't project far through this dense foliage. The men were less than twenty feet away. That was horrifying. She and Thomas had almost walked into two unknown men. As close as they were to the fighting these could be rebels or Frederick's men. Either way they wouldn't be safe. Even the rebels whose families Melene and her associates were feeding and clothing might shoot first and ask questions later with how jumpy and outnumbered they were.

Should they backtrack?

The men weren't moving and neither was Thomas. She imagined any movement from her or Thomas might be heard and investigated. She prayed she and Thomas could be safe, and could know when to make their getaway. But what about their family? They couldn't desert them to whoever these men were.

She could clearly see the guy facing her as the other man held up a cell phone, showing him something on it. The man was tall and had sharp features, paler skin with dark eyes and hair. He would probably be considered classically handsome, but Melene could see cruelty in his features. With all she'd seen and experienced in her charity work throughout the world, she'd come to recognize ruthlessness and steer far away from it.

She tugged on Thomas' arm but he didn't move.

The man holding the phone explained slowly in accented English, "The yacht is, 'My Lady'. It leaves Marina Lubmin at nineteen hundred hours. Chancellor Kohl and staff on board. Your bombs must be set *before* leaves."

Melene's eyes widened. They were planning to assassinate Germany's most powerful leader. It was common knowledge the chancellor truly led the country. These men had to be Frederick's. Would they take on Germany before Poland? Were the threats against Poland only a smoke screen? Was Frederick strong enough to fight on two fronts?

Melene would pass the information on and hope the right people could stop the assassination attempt. Her body went cold and she shivered. What she and Thomas had just overheard was their death sentence if these men discovered them. She yearned to back away and tug Thomas with her, but was afraid to make any noise.

"Do not presume to instruct me on my mission," the Brit sneered at the German. What was it about that voice? That face?

Her horror tripled and her body shook so hard she was afraid she'd hit into a tree branch or something. Melene recognized who the Brit was. General Carl Phillip. She'd seen him on television, on the right side of King Frederick. Defected from Britain's army and now a hired mercenary who Frederick had deemed one of his generals. Phillip had a reputation as a cold-blooded killer and a womanizer who didn't take no for an answer.

Her pulse raced and ice pricked at her neck. What kind of a nightmarish mess had they stumbled on to? How could she get Thomas to safety? She prayed desperately for some miracle that she and Thomas would stay safe and that their family wouldn't appear and blunder onto these men like they had.

Against all she hoped and prayed, the two men started walking in their direction. Her stomach dropped. No, no, no! There was no way the men wouldn't bump right into them on the path.

The man with the phone was groveling loudly his apologies and that of course the general was "the expert".

Thomas glanced back at her, the fear in his eyes palpable. "Run," he mouthed.

Melene nodded. Running was their only option. Melene could run fast and so could Thomas. She often organized foot races with the youth and Thomas was one of the few who could beat her consistently.

But what if they shot them?

They had no choice. Running was their only option and she knew it. Melene pivoted and took off at a sprint. Thomas was so close to her backside, he clipped her heel. She stumbled but kept going.

Low curses came from behind and then the dreaded footsteps taking up pursuit. Melene upped her pace through the moon-dappled forest and thankfully Thomas kept up and neither of them tripped or ran into a tree.

The men weren't as fast and she could sense them falling behind. That was the only good news of the night.

Would they shoot at them? She flinched just imagining them pulling their guns and taking aim. She'd been in many dangerous situations throughout the past few years, but a known murderer, the right-hand man of the most evil man on the planet, chasing her through a dark forest with a fourteen-year old relying on her to save him, might top them all.

She burst out of the forest trail and almost flew off the ledge and to the rocks and ocean below them. Grabbing a tree branch she whirled around and slid onto the ocean path. Thomas stayed right behind her. Her brain screamed at her to slow down so she didn't plunge off the cliff, but she'd risk splatting on the rocks over being caught by General Phillip.

Thomas panted for air behind her and she hated that they had no coverage now they were out of the trees. The half moon had seemed a blessing earlier. Now it felt like a curse. Out here on this ledge the men could pick them off like ducks.

Luckily no gunshots yet. Did that just mean the men knew they'd catch them eventually, and they wanted to know who they were and what she and Thomas had heard before they tortured and killed them? The men also hadn't yelled or called out to them. It was eerie. Especially as the thud of their heavier footsteps seemed to grow louder. She couldn't afford to stop or slow down.

Melene had been dubbed "sunshine" and "sweetness" by children and their parents in different languages the world over. She felt like neither right now. "Horror" and "darkness" were all she could feel.

The trail split in front of her. Melene could stay on the ridge and run the half mile back to their camp. She and Thomas were faster, but the men would easily follow them and catch them when they reached camp.

More people might mean safety, but their camp had no military support or healthy men between the ages of fifteen and sixty. The men were either fighting with the rebels or they'd been killed or conscripted into Frederick's army. A ruthless leader like General Phillip might kill more than just her and Thomas if she led him to the refugee camp. She couldn't willingly put those people on that man's radar.

She squinted into the darkness and could make out the other trail. It led down through craggy rocks and to the beach and ocean. Choosing that direction looked to be a completely idiotic choice. If she remembered right the beach wrapped around the cliffs and back to some restaurants, bars, and shops, but she wasn't certain if this was that spot. If it was an isolated beach they could possibly swim to get away, but more likely she would trap herself and Thomas. The men behind them would easily extract their information and then kill them. She knew her path in life was risky but she'd never been in this deep of mortal peril and usually the people she was serving protected and revered her.

She said a prayer for direction, and darted down toward the beach.

"Melene," Thomas hissed from behind her, obviously thinking it was the wrong choice. She half expected him to go the other direction, but he followed her.

Dumb, dumb, dumb. Why had she gone this way? Was she following inspiration or desperation? It was really hard to know when she was terrified and running for her life.

She scrambled down a rock and glanced back. The general was at the top of the trail, his cohort next to him. The light of the moon glinted off the sharp planes of his face. He gave her a smile that made her skin crawl. He was going to enjoy trapping and torturing her.

Tripping over a rock, she went down hard, scraping her knees and palms on the uneven boulders. She cried out.

"Okay?" Thomas asked, helping her back to her feet.

No! She wasn't okay and he wasn't going to be okay. Please help, she begged anyone in heaven who had a spare minute.

"Yep," she grunted, blood trickling down her knees.

The small injury was the worst of her concerns as she heard pebbles being dislodged from above. The two men easily followed them down the steep trail.

Melene hurried as fast as she dared. General Phillip wasn't in a hurry. He thought he had them trapped and he was probably the type who enjoyed toying with his prey and making them suffer before he mercilessly tortured and then killed them.

He was most likely right in assuming she was trapped, but Melene refused to give up. She'd felt inspired to go this way and she was trusting in that. She would pray they could run along the beach and get lost in the restaurants or bars that would still be open around the cliff, or worst case if the beach didn't continue around the bend like she was visualizing, they'd swim to escape him. She would focus positivity on living another day to serve and lift and give love and most importantly on keeping Thomas alive. *If not please let Grammy Larue forgive me for "gettin' meself killed in them darn jungles".* She almost smiled thinking of her outspoken grandmother back home in Colorado. At least her family was safe back at home. On the hard days that always helped her get through.

She scrambled down the trail and finally skirted around the last rock. Sinking in the thick sand she plunged to the left, praying and praying for protection and an escape route. The cliffs rose around her and she recognized instantly she'd made an idiotic, death-certificate mistake.

This wasn't the beach that connected to the restaurants. It was a beautiful, sheltered cove. Probably paradise to anyone on a bright, sunny day, who wasn't being hunted, and hadn't just trapped themselves and an innocent boy with a homicidal British maniac and his companion.

Glancing back, she could see General Phillip easing down the last half of the incline. He caught her gaze on him and gave her a wink and a grin. Her stomach churned. He was laughing at her.

"Thomas," she hissed, untying and ripping off her shoes. "We have to swim. It's our only chance."

"I no swim," he said, shaking his head, his dark eyes wide with fear. He looked as miserable as a teenager facing death could look.

Ah, no. Thomas was from a mountainous village and hadn't even seen the ocean before coming to their refugee camp. Why had she stupidly assumed any fourteen-year old boy would know how to swim?

"I'll tow you," she encouraged, grabbing his hand and yanking him toward the water.

Thomas looked as horrified as going into the ocean as he did of facing the men. But he obediently slid his shoes off and let her pull him across the beach and into the softly breaking waves.

"Stop." The cold command and cocking of two pistols came from behind them. Melene had the impression nobody argued with that man and she could only imagine he was accurate with his instruments of death.

Melene and Thomas whirled to face the men. They were at the bottom of the rocks, not stepping onto the beach as if it would sully their boots. They each held pistols in their hands, pointed right at Thomas. How did they instinctively know she would protect Thomas?

Melene's pulse raced out of control. Could they dive into the water and swim away without getting shot? If they could both swim they had a one in a million chance. With her pulling and towing a boy afraid of the water they were dead.

She prayed desperately for some help or inspiration. With no idea what to pray for she simply repeated in her mind, *Please, please, please help ... somehow.*

Thomas sweetly stepped in front of her and put his hands out. "No kill the lady," he yelled.

General Phillip let out a cultured laugh that was echoed by the other man's more guttural chuckle. Their laughter cut off abruptly, as if they'd cued it. The only sound was the lapping of the waves and all of their panting breaths of air from the run of no escape.

"It will be with pleasure that I shoot both of you between the eyes," General Phillip said as if telling them he was going to eat fish for dinner. He made no move to step closer, knowing they had no escape. "After you explain precisely who you are, how you knew to eavesdrop on us, and what exactly you overheard."

"Why would we tell you anything if you're going to kill us?" Melene hurled at him, stepping to Thomas' side despite his attempts to stay in front of her. There was no hope of escape. Despair stronger than the darkest night surged in her chest. Could she protect Thomas? Not if he couldn't swim.

"An American?" General Phillip's brows rose.

"Yes," she said, tilting her chin up. "I have American military protection and you will be swiftly brought to justice if you murder us."

He laughed again. It was dark and cold. "Come now, my cheeky and lovely American. We both know your cowardly excuse for a President isn't willing to rock the boat and risk nuclear winter. There might be a few military special ops units hoping to sneak into the action, but they wouldn't waste their time with a citizen who stuck her nose in business were it doesn't belong. Your life is of little consequence to your military or your country." He looked her over and her unease battled with the despair. "But you are an extremely beautiful and fit woman. You want a deal, love? Everybody likes a deal." He nodded as if she were agreeing.

"No, thank you," Melene said primly.

"No touch Melene!" Thomas yelled in support. It sickened her that at such a young age he instantly knew what the general was after.

"You haven't even listened to my deal." He didn't give them a chance to respond but went on, "I will keep you near my side beautiful American, as long as I continue to fancy you," he licked his lips, "and you are only cheeky in the appropriate moments." He smiled. "And I won't even kill the boy."

Melene sucked in a breath. The thought of going anywhere near this man made her skin crawl, but if he'd truly spare Thomas she would give herself up, and pray somehow she'd be rescued before he ... she couldn't think about *that* and who in the world could rescue her from the likes of this monster?

"I will have to cut his tongue out," General Phillip explained casually, "to make certain he squeaks to no one what he saw or heard tonight."

"No!" Melene cried out.

General Phillip lifted his left palm up in a sign of peace. His right hand still clutched the pistol aimed at them so his sign of peace was a little hypocritical. "It is a very generous offer for a couple of spies."

"We no spies," Thomas spit out. "Melene protects and loves the children."

"How very kind of her," General Phillip said in what he probably thought was a charming voice. "Now she will have the privilege of protecting and loving me."

Melene's stomach curdled like she'd drank a gallon of rancid milk. She grasped Thomas' hand and prayed desperately. Was there any other option? She couldn't see one. Tilting her chin up she said, "I will go with you."

"No!" Thomas yelled. "No!"

Phillip smiled creepily.

"But you will not cut Thomas' tongue out. He is a very staunch Catholic and will keep his word. He will swear to us by heaven above that he will not breathe one word of what happened to me or what he overheard, and you can trust that he will not."

Thomas stared at her as if she were insane. The look on the general and the other man's faces echoed it. Not even Thomas believed his promise to a devil like General Phillip was going to stick. As brave as this kid was, he might even tell the general to cut his tongue out. He could still write down what had happened, but she didn't want to point that out.

Despair coursed through her. She was going to become this despicable man's property and Thomas would lose his tongue. It was all too horrific to imagine. She'd been in many a bad or awkward spot but nothing as desperate as this.

There was no sound but the soft waves as General Phillip looked her over as if he already owned her, a disgusting smile on his lips.

She heard a soft splash and turned to look as something disturbed the surface of the water.

Melene was certain she was hallucinating. A shape rose out of the water not two feet behind her. No one said anything as they all stared in shock. It was a man. A man dressed in a black scuba diving suit complete with tanks on his back, a face mask, a diving belt with weights, a knife, and a gun on it, and a ventilator in his mouth.

He pulled the ventilator out and grinned at her, water sparkling off his handsome face and dark hair. "Hi, Melene."

Melene couldn't for the life of her fathom how Aiden Delta, her high school buddy, and now an accomplished Navy SEAL, had just materialized out of the ocean at the exact moment she needed a knight in shining ... scuba gear.

"Aiden?" she whispered.

His blue eyes twinkled from behind the mask. "In a bit of trouble, are we?"

Her own eyes widened. She'd temporarily forgotten about the men ready to kidnap her and cut out Thomas' tongue. She whirled around and General Phillip and his buddy were now edging across the sand toward them.

"I'd suggest you stop, and put down the guns," Aiden said to them, lifting his goggles up onto his forehead so she could see his handsome face better. How in the world had he come up out of the water like he was Aqua Man?

General Phillip chuckled. "You've lost the plot. Who is going to stop me, you barmy git all by yourself?"

Aiden gestured casually behind him. "My *mates*," he mimicked Phillip's accent. "Don't mess with me you mangy twit."

Melene was terrified that Aiden had lost his mind and just signed his own death sentence trying to bluff his way into rescuing her, and throwing English slang in to tick General Phillip off even more. Aiden had always been an overconfident tease and she wouldn't put it past him to try to bluff his way through a situation like this.

Suddenly dark shapes starting rising out of the ocean, four, no five men, and they all had guns in their hands. A sleek boat cruised around the side of the cliff. Two men manned the boat. One was in the driver's seat, the other one stood at the bow lofting a huge automatic-looking gun right at the general.

"Is it your hour to die General Phillip?" Aiden asked. "Or would you like to head back up that trail and continue your evil deeds for a few more days?"

General Phillip glowered at them. "You Americans have no rights and no presence that is accepted here. I have eyes and ears everywhere on this continent. I will hunt all of you down, slit your barmy throats, and take the woman as my prize."

"That was a lovely and inspiring speech." Aiden's gaze turned steely. "Right now I'd suggest you set your guns down and slither back up the mountain like the snakes you are."

The man didn't move. A gun fired and the sand next to General Phillip exploded, showering crystals of sand on him and his man. Thomas cheered and the German man cursed, but nobody else said a word. Melene had no idea who had fired. She prayed desperately the general would listen to Aiden and leave. Her heart beat so high and fast she couldn't swallow and hoped she wouldn't be called upon to talk.

General Phillip slowly set his gun down and the other guy followed suit. They backed toward the rocks. Melene panted for air. Would he really just leave?

He pointed a finger at Aiden. "I will find you ... squid," he threatened.

Aiden tilted his head. "You know, it's humorous when the Army or Air Force guys throw that term at us, but I don't like it coming out of your mouth." He pulled a knife off of his belt. He flipped the knife open and pointed it at the general. "Maybe your tongue is the one that needs to be cut out. Then nobody would have to be subject to your vile, filthy lies any longer."

The general's eyes widened at the threat and suddenly he was hurrying up the mountainside.

Aiden winked at Melene, closed the knife, and fastened it back on his diving belt. "Bullies never like a taste of their own medicine." He lowered his voice. "Let's go. He won't give us much lead time and sadly the pathetic worm wasn't bluffing."

Melene was shaking with the fear of what could've been, but if she understood Aiden correctly General Phillip would track them down, and he would bring an army next time.

Aiden pushed through the water to her and wrapped an arm around her waist. The warm pressure of him close somehow dispelled the fear and the darkness. She looked up into his handsome face and breathed out, "Thank you." She wanted to gush about him being a hero and if she were being honest she'd love to give him a kiss of gratitude, but she and Aiden weren't romantically involved and she could still feel the danger pulsing outside of the circle of Aiden's arms. Sadly there was no time to gush over him, catch up on family back home right now, or see if there was a romantic spark with this incredible Navy SEAL who'd just saved her from a fate worse than death.

There might never be time for any of that. General Phillip would be back, and he'd fulfill his threats. She shuddered, and clung to Aiden as they made their way to the boat.

Find *Compromised* on Amazon.

Also by Cami Checketts

Delta Family Romances

Deceived

Abandoned

Committed

Betrayed

Devoted

Compromised

Endangered

Accepted

Returned

Devastated

Famous Friends Romances

Loving the Firefighter

Loving the Athlete

Loving the Rancher

Loving the Coach

Loving the Contractor

Loving the Sheriff

Loving the Entertainer

The Hidden Kingdom Romances

Royal Secrets

Royal Security

Royal Doctor

Royal Mistake

Royal Courage

Royal Pilot

Royal Imposter

Royal Baby

Royal Battle

Royal Fake Fiancé

Secret Valley Romance

Sister Pact

Marriage Pact

Christmas Pact

Survive the Romance

Romancing the Treasure

Romancing the Escape

Romancing the Boat

Romancing the Mountain

Romancing the Castle

Romancing the Extreme Adventure

Romancing the Island

Romancing the River

Romancing the Spartan Race

Mystical Lake Resort Romance

Only Her Undercover Spy

Only Her Cowboy

Only Her Best Friend

Only Her Blue-Collar Billionaire

About the Author

Cami is a part-time author, part-time exercise consultant, part-time housekeeper, full-time wife, and overtime mother of four adorable boys. Sleep and relaxation are fond memories. She's never been happier.

Join Cami's VIP list to find out about special deals, giveaways and new releases and receive a free copy of *Rescued by Love: Park City Firefighter Romance* by clicking here.

cami@camichecketts.com

www.camichecketts.com

Made in United States
Orlando, FL
30 March 2023